PENGUIN BOOKS

# WINDS OF WAR

Mica De Leon is a Filipino writer of swoony romance comedy novels and SFF novels. She is the author of the romance book, *Love on The Second Read*, published by Penguin Random House SEA. She has won the Don Carlos Palanca Awards for Literature in 2019 and 2022 for her essays on romance, feminism, history, fantasy, and the Filipino identity in the aftermath of Martial Law and the 2022 presidential elections in the Philippines. She likes walking on the beach, dogs, cats, swoony and spicy romance novels, long epic SFF novels, and Taylor Swift.

Connect with her on Instagram, Tiktok, Threads, and Twitter: @micadeleonwrites

Also by Mica De Leon

*Love on the Second Read (2023)*

# Winds of War

## Seedmage Cycle Book 1

Mica De Leon

PENGUIN BOOKS
An imprint of Penguin Random House

PENGUIN BOOKS

USA | Canada | UK | Ireland | Australia
New Zealand | India | South Africa | China | Southeast Asia

Penguin Books is part of the Penguin Random House group of companies
whose addresses can be found at global.penguinrandomhouse.com

Published by Penguin Random House SEA Pte Ltd
9, Changi South Street 3, Level 08-01,
Singapore 486361

First published in Penguin Books by Penguin Random House SEA 2024



10 9 8 7 6 5 4 3 2 1



ISBN 9789815144284

Typeset in Garamond by MAP Systems, Bengaluru, India



www.penguin.sg

*For you, may your life be lived in love.*

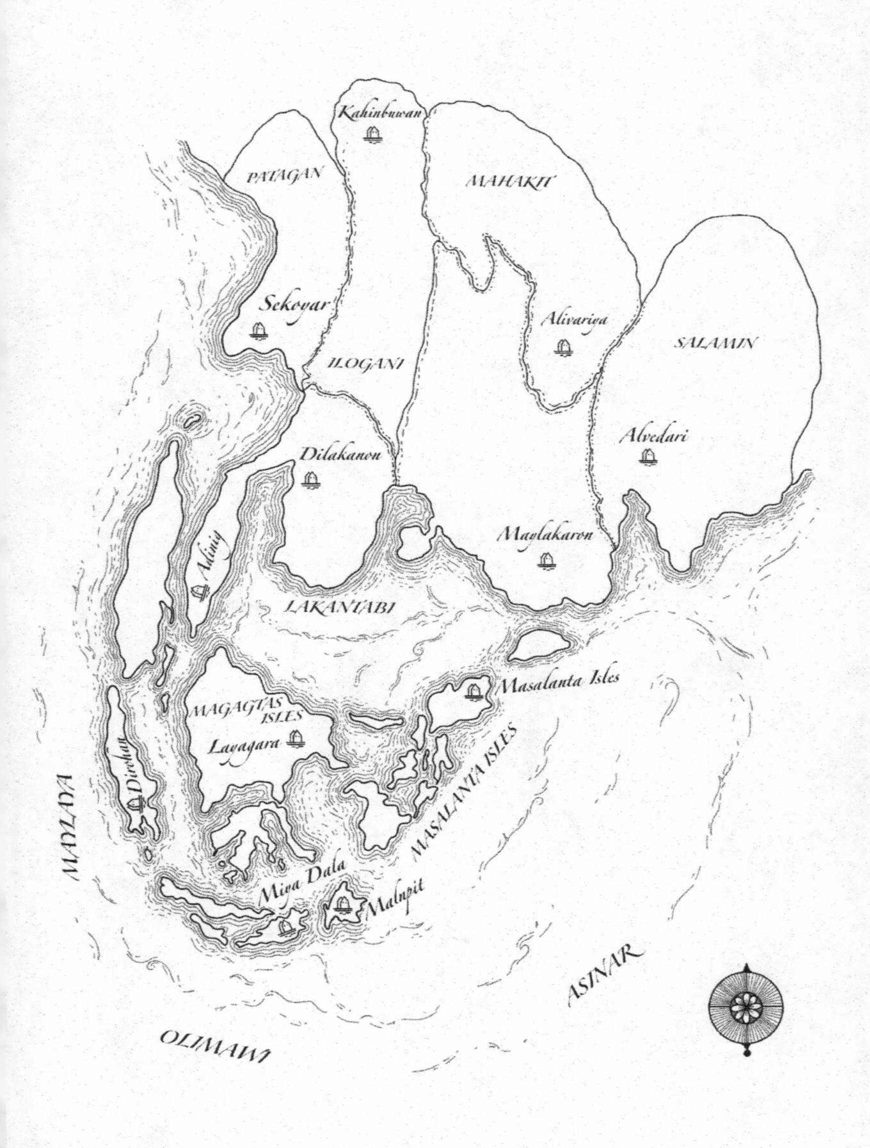
Kahinbuwan
PATAGAN
MAHAKIT
Sekoyar
Alivariya
SALAMIN
ILOGANI
Alvedari
Dilakanon
Maylakaron
Adinig
LAKANTABI
Masalanta Isles
MAGAGTAS ISLES
Lagagara
MASALANTA ISLES
Direhan
MAYLADA
Miya Dala
Malupit
ASINAR
OLIMAWI

# Notes

- **KAYUMALON:** A powerful kingdom with ten provinces, occupied by various noble houses (the leaders of which are from the direct bloodline of Maragtas the Conqueror), Dayo servants, and strangelord (non-human) races.
- **KAYUMAN :** The common language and the people of the Kayumalon kingdom.
- **DATUS:** The leaders of the ten great noble Houses of Kayumalon are called this.
- **DAYO:** The people who are the serving class in the Kayuman society. Identified by their pale skin. Work as manual labour, and on plantations to cultivate the seeds from which the oils that allow seedmages to harness their magic are made.
- **STRANGELORDS:** There are four strangelord races-
  - **Dalaket:** The tree folk.
  - **Tikalbang:** Horse-humanoids, akin to centaurs.

  - **Asinari:** The merfolk.
  - **Asuwan:** The undying.
- **REDS:** Soldiers of the Kalasag Army of Kayumalon who've sworn fealty to the monarch.
- **THE SEVEN SKYWORLD GODS:** They are also known as seedgods (which then use humans as vessels to exist in the earthly realm). They are essentially pieces of one big god that was broken apart. The seven gods are as follows:
  - **Dirigma** - Red moon
  - **Haliya** - Orange moon
  - **Sinag** - Yellow moon
  - **Tala** - Green moon
  - **Asin** - Blue moon
  - **Buwan** - Indigo moon
  - **Bihag** - Violet moon
- **SEEDMAGES:** Those who can harness the divine power using seedoil.
- **THE MAGIC SYSTEMS:** There are three magic systems used by the mages. They are listed as below:
  - **Vitaulurgy:** The main magic system that reaches for the origins of seedmagic from which Theochemy and Germachemy branches out of.
  - **Theochemy:** The (unstudied) magic used to fuse souls with a seedgod.
  - **Germachemy:** The magic that seedmages can harness using seedshooters. The different powers correspond to their respective colours, listed as below-
    - Red- Increases adrenaline.

- Orange- Increases and strengthens muscle mass.
- Yellow- Releases pheromones that serve different purposes.
- Green- Allows you to manipulate other's vision by interfering with light.
- Blue- Used to invoke darker mood, can be used as a depressant.
- Indigo- Helps repair cells and accelerates healing.
- Violet- Increases muscle and skin elasticity.

# Dramatis Personae

## KAYUMALON

***THE HOUSES OF KAYUMALON***: There are four great houses; House Maylakan, House Laya, House Payapas, and House Layon—and several minor houses that serve the Datus as bannermen. Three minor houses feature significantly here: House Talim, House Dalasay, and House Layag.

## THE GREAT KAYUMAN HOUSES

### HOUSE MAYLAKAN

(LAKANLUPA)

KALEM MAYLAKAN: The king preceding Dumas.
DUMA MAYLAKAN: The current monarch (wife: LIGAYA LAYA-MAYLAKAN).
DAKILA MAYLAKAN (*Talim*): The second-born prince, allegedly the queen's bastard.

DANGAL MAYLAKAN: The first-born prince, child of Duma and Ligaya.

## HOUSE LAYA

(MAYLAYA)

PATAS LAYA: Also known as the Obsidian Datu (wife: DIWA LAYON-LAYA).
KALEM LAYA: Patas and Diwa's son.

## HOUSE LAYON

(MARAGTAS ISLES)

MARALITA LAYON: A member of the Kalasag Army, works under Dakila's command.

## THE LESSER KAYUMAN HOUSES

### HOUSE TALIM

PANDAY TALIM: Kalem's aide and bodyguard.

## *THE SEED GODS*

DIAN: A yellow maya, Goddess of the East Wind.
DAMU: An indigo turtle, God of the Earth.
SITAN: A violet-black raven, God of Death.

## *MASALANTA ISLAND*

TIYAGO MASALANTA: A Dayo labourer working on the Masalanta seedplantation.

FERIDINAN MASALANTA: Brother of Tiyago, a Dayo labourer working on the Masalanta seedplantation.

REJEENA MASALANTA: A Dayo labourer working on the seedplantation.

GALENYA: Healer working on the Masalanta seedplantation.

YIN'S FATHER: An ex-military Kayuman, now working as foreman on the Masalanta seedplantation.

## TUKIKUNI

THE SPIDER EMPRESS

## THE SPIDER'S CHILDREN

JINWUN

SEYO

HANABI

HONGSU

GAMU

JIJIN

JEONJUN - A foot soldier in the Tukikuni army.

GONCHUN - JinWun's husband.

# Prologue

The Death God's shadow darkened all doorsteps. It was only a matter of time.

The Shadow took his time going to his mission location. He hated this part. The waiting. The long stretch of nothing leading up to an inevitable spectacle. He hated it more that he had no say in this, the wanton demise of a family before their time, by his divine hand.

That was his life now. Bouts of hate between bouts of nothing. His powers were merely tools, the shadows that answered his beckoning were simply pawns, following the orders of the cruel hand who owned this Shadow's soul.

No, the Shadow was no god, but he was a bastard, borne by a slave to a king. The spirit that followed him around, the black silvery mass that took the shape of a raven. Now *this* was the god that inhabited his body.

***'Is this death justified?'*** The raven asked, floating around his hooded head like it was an actual bird, a raven the size of a common maya. It had become a ritual for both god and host to ask this question before every mission. The Shadow sometimes pretended to know the answer, especially when the victim was a vile character. Other times, the Shadow was brave enough to tell the truth; that no one deserved an abrupt end to life, and certainly not by his hand.

*'It is not, Sitan,'* the Shadow answered as he approached the looming iron gate of the mansion, which was at least five times his height. This was an answer he knew for sure, a truth.

***'Who are they?'*** Sitan asked as it shifted its form into a dark cloud that enveloped the Shadow's body. He closed his violet eyes, the moonslight painting his pale face in outlines interrupted by glowing black veins. He breathed in the night air and stretched his neck this way and that, feeling his own body morphing with the raven's, their combined forms becoming the Shadow God that mortals feared. Sitan—the black raven—was the God of Death and decay after all.

When the transformation was complete, he stared up at the mansion beyond the gates, paltry protection against divine intervention. It was a beautiful mansion, a good home that housed a good family, with its solid stone walls and sweeping red pagoda rooftops; with its wide-open windows on all five floors, letting in the warm east wind. This part of the country was closer to the winter lands and therefore the farthest from the heat and rage of the capital cities and the perpetually sunny, summer isles of Kayumalon. Even in the chill, the mansion looked like a warm, inviting home, with a hearth in the very base where the family gathered—the family he was about to murder.

The Shadow always made a point of knowing who his victims were. Though he was an executioner, he was not the judge who decided it was their time to die. That power, his power, belonged to a mortal who thought himself bigger than a god.

The people who made this home were called the Payapas. It was ironic—or perhaps poetic justice—that their death would usher in an age of war for this country. Their bloodline was next in line to the throne, whose current occupant was on the verge of being dethroned. The king had kept his Shadow hidden, tucked safely away, used only when absolutely necessary. The Shadow was a weapon that couldn't be used lightly, a double-edged sword, a calamity walking.

The king must be desperate to order a massacre—this massacre especially.

*'House Payapa were pacifists. Datu Payapa rarely took sides in the Congress Of Datus,'* the Shadow began as he pushed forward through the iron bars, which curled up and cracked into rusted metal and then crumbled into red dust upon contact with his body. *'He rarely forced his principles and beliefs on others, but he lived by them—his entire family did, from his ageing mother, the king's younger sister, down to his great, great grandchildren. Datu Payapa never threw his weight around even if it was within his power to do so. He would have solved every problem of the country if he'd done so, but that would have made him many enemies along the way. So he always chose the peaceful path. He always found a compromise that satisfied everybody.'* He left a trail of black smoke billowing behind him as he walked, slipping past two guards, who watched the scene in horror and disbelief before one of them ran to get help. The other stayed and lit his veins red.

**'Why does the master want him and his entire clan dead?'** The raven asked, its essence swirling within the Shadow's body. The Shadow crested the hill, following the paved pathway to the mansion, just as a guard rushed up to him with a raised sword.

The Shadow stopped and waited for the guard, shaking his head impatiently, warning the poor soul that resistance was futile. He didn't want to kill any more than necessary today.

*'The master was losing. He doesn't like losing,'* he answered the raven simply and looked the guard in the eye. 'I'll spare your life if you run now.'

The guard's veins blazed orange and he launched his entire body toward the Shadow's human-shaped smokey mass. The poor guard merely passed through the smoke, exiting as a blackened skeleton, which disintegrated in the wind as it fell to the ground.

The Shadow sighed and turned toward the thundering of boots running up to him, slowing as they watched their comrade perish under the Shadow's hands, without even being able to put up a semblance of a fight. The echo of a loud horn blowing into the night filled the air. Immediately, the lights within the mansion went on, outlining the silhouettes of people running to and fro within the structure.

***'They're escaping,'*** Sitan said, but the Shadow didn't move, though he felt his master's command rattling his bones. ***'You're not giving chase?'*** The bird waited for the Shadow to make a move. ***'You want them to escape.'*** It was a statement, rife not with kindness or sympathy, but with accusation.

*'I want to give them a chance,'* the Shadow said as the guards surrounded him. Giving his victims a shot at survival was a way to assuage his guilt over a senseless, undeserved death.

***'But we're inevitable.'***

*'Eventually,'* the Shadow answered, focusing on the guards, taunting them by pulling out a sword with his gloved hand.

It was a plain iron sword, a toy compared to the brand of death that he could deliver solely with his godvessel, his magic, his curse. 'Death comes to us all, but only sooner if we invite it. I'll spare your life if you run now.'

Sometimes, the Shadow thought he had too much faith in mortals, so much that he overestimated their ability to make sensible choices, that he underestimated their potential to be imbeciles in a crisis. Of course, the guards ran up to him, swords raised, veins lit, battle-cry echoing in the night.

The Shadow sighed. Too much faith for his own good. He threw down his sword, morphing his human-shaped body, exploding into a cloud of death right before a sword sliced the black air. The first guard's body disintegrated to dust before the iron had a chance to hit the ground. It fell with a desultory clang, a dying song of metal that was bound to follow its wielder's fate it turned into dust as another guard followed his comrade's fate. They followed each other to death, one after another, falling again and again and again. Finding nothing within the black mass but shadow and smoke and darkness. Only the Shadow within could see them. Only the Shadow within stood witness to their last dying breath, their last fight for life, *their last.*

Enough people had died before the remaining guards realized that they stood no chance against the Shadow, and those who had more sense than the others dropped their weapons and ran for their lives. Those who remained stood their ground, bolstered by stupid courage, and watched him with abject horror.

'Your deaths don't matter to these people,' the Shadow said. 'But it matters to someone else, if not to you. Don't throw your life away.'

More fled, but not all of them. The few who remained circled him, prowling—like a snake around a bird of prey. The Shadow noted that their tattoos designated them as officers. Too bad he was worse than a bird of prey; he was the predator that spelled their death.

The Shadow felt the command overpowering whatever volition he had left and the cloud expanded around him, reaching the last of the remaining guards, who decayed and disintegrated, despite the Shadow's best efforts. They disappeared too fast; too fast for the Shadow to be able to put up a fight against the divine bonds that controlled him.

The Shadow didn't bother going into the mansion. The family would have already been alerted of his arrival. It wasn't every day that Death gave his victims a head start. The Shadow hoped that they had used the time he'd given them wisely.

They hadn't. He found the family later, fleeing through the thicket of trees behind the mansion, along a secret pathway that was concealed behind a hidden door in the cellars.

The oldest of them, Datu Payapa, came forward, shielding his family from the Shadow. 'Who is your master, demon?' He raised a spherical glass glowlamp in a net hanging from a hook. 'Is it the king?'

The Shadow gave the old man the courtesy of allowing him to see his assassin in the flesh, allowing the raven to separate from his body and perch on his shoulder, 'Does it matter who?' The light shone on his pale face cracked with black veins.

'No.' The old man looked over his shoulder at his family then back at the Shadow, shaking his head, 'I suppose not.' He lowered his lamp and handed it to the boy standing with his hand on the pommel of his sword behind Datu Payapa. 'Spare them. It's me you want dead.'

'It's not me who wants you dead.' The Shadow offered a hand to the Datu, poison smoke billowing tendrils of black shadows upward from it. 'My command is to spare no one, but I can make it so that no one suffers.'

The old man gave him a long hard look as if trying to convince himself that there were other options, other pathways for them to take where Death let them escape; compromises he could offer to convince Death to let them live another day. 'Will there be pain?'

There was no compromising with Death. The Shadow shook his head.

'Will you allow us to say our goodbyes?'

The Shadow did.

There was no crying, only apologies, only words left unsaid in a long life, only regrets, only gratitude for a life shared through pain and bliss. When they were done, the family stood tall against their murderer, holding hands, accepting their fate.

'We're ready,' the Datu said and reached for the Shadow's outstretched hand.

The raven pierced the Shadow's body from behind, and they exploded into a cloud of smoke. The Payapas disintegrated almost instantaneously—black, white, and grey debris and dust floating like petals falling from trees at the seam between dry and wet seasons.

When it was done and the raven had unfused with his body to perch on his shoulder, the Shadow was alone again, but he was unsettled. His orders were to spare no one, and when the master gave the command, it was absolute. It was inimitable. It was inevitable. Just as death was for mortals.

***'One of them survived,'*** the raven Sitan said, taking flight from the Shadow's shoulder and hovering over his head, the command thrumming within the Shadow's body, urging, ordering, forcing him to finish his mission.

Later, he found the child in the playroom, cowering and hidden under the floorboards. The last of the Payapas, the last of this peaceful family. The boy was crying and looking at the Shadow towering over him with pleading eyes. Like his father, this Payapa begged for a compromise. Like his father, this Payapa tried to negotiate with Death.

But there was no negotiating with Death and whatever humanity the Shadow had left in him screamed at him to let the boy go, let him live, let him be the last living proof that his family ever lived. Of course, even his humanity was no longer his.

The command rattled in his very core, and he and the raven together became a cloud of death again, floating in tendrils that crawled up to the boy. He kept his promise to the child's father—there was no pain. Only death.

Death had no purpose. It was the end. Not a goal, but an inevitability. Not a defeat, but not a victory either. It was simply ceasing. No more. No less.

It was too much power for one small man.

The winds of war blew a battle horn in the air around the Shadow, and, alone, lonely, and loathing himself for what he had done, the Death God's mortal host decided that it was finally time for him to die.

# ACT 1

# Chapter 1

## Yin

*Six Months Ago*

Seven gods of light raced each other across the Skyworld realms, and a girl stood on unsteady ground, trying to read the sky as the ship flew under it.

Yin's pale face was painted with the colours of the seven moons—celestial gods of Kayuman myths chasing after the King of Gods, the Morningstar—trailing stardust in their wake. She knew this story because her mother sang the lullaby to her when she was a girl. Her mother once sang it to a Kayuman boy she served as a wet nurse back before Yin was born.

Yin hummed the tune as their flying Dalaket cargo ship approached its destination, drawing lines from one coconut-sized moon in the sky to another. It was nighttime, but the seven moons gave the world an unusual tinge of colour that wasn't quite dark, but wasn't white daylight either. On good nights, the sky was an artist's canvas of light. On the worst nights—such as now—the sky was eerie, threatening and inauspicious, an artwork of blood red, sharp lapis lazuli blue and moss green splashed across the canvas.

Kayumalon was the country smack-dab in the middle of the equator, the line that divided the world between the northern and southern hemisphere, so it got the best of summer and the worst of monsoon.

Standing on the deck, Yin thought that this was the best part of always leaving home and flying with the gods. Sometimes she imagined that if she reached her hands far enough, she'd catch one of the gods in the palm of her hands. Sometimes, she imagined that they spoke to her in her dreams.

She could feel the heat of the Morningstar's rays on her skin even after it had set, darkening the horizon, but it did little else to her pale skin that was wanting of colour. Try as she might to bathe in the morningstarlight, her skin remained pale, paler than it had any right to be, being who, or what, she was. The Morningstar would no sooner burn her before she turned the same rich colour as Kayuman nobles, or any Kayuman really—like her father. She got her skin from her Dayo mother, who had died in the last home they had left behind.

'We need to keep moving,' her father had said, her mother's body not even ashes in the wind, before getting on the next flying Dalaket ship to some other plantation island many years ago. *Did her father even mourn her mother?*

She propped her elbows on the railings of the wooden ship as it descended into Masalanta Island's docks, her long, dark hair billowing in the wind. The air was humid, it hung heavily with the sickeningly sweet scent of mangoes and saltwater.

Like most island plantations she'd lived in, Masalanta had seedfields that stretched out in long rows of green, between twisting tracks of dirt and grass-speckled pathways that went over the rolling hills cradling the valley.

The Dayo village lay at the foot of that valley—quiet, calm, homey, with quaint homes of crooked, grey stone walls brown hay rooftops, orange wood doors, and wide-open windows. The Kayuman noblemen's houses were smooth white stone structures with sweeping black pagoda rooftops and gleaming metal-gilded corners. They were built closer to the harbor where ships were moored and waiting for the island's harvest. The howling winds of a typhoon may rush through the small streets, but the mountains and hills protected them from the worst of it—houses stayed standing, and the harvest kept coming. And everywhere, the sweet, nectarine scent of seedmagic hung heavily in the air and clung to their clothes and hair.

This was the island that was known as the biggest seedplantation island in the south and therefore had the largest population of Dayo laborers. Yin would blend right in, hiding in plain sight, her father said, not bothering to explain at all why she needed to hide.

'You there! Dayo! Go below deck now!' The Dalaket captain bellowed, voice rough against the whistling wind as the ship descended rapidly. He meant her, but she ignored him.

She was the only Dayo on the deck of the ship. Most of the Dayo servants were kept in the hull before landing to prevent escapes. Ships like these employed Dalaket and

Kayuman officers and left the grunt work to a handful of servants they bought and traded in different docks.

Yin, on the other hand, wasn't a property of this ship. She was half-Kayuman on her father's side, and therefore had more rights than the average Dayo.

That didn't deter the ageing captain though. Her perceived obstinacy to ignore him seemed to ruffle his feathers—or rather his green and greying leaves. The Dalaket tree people were the most stubborn of the strangelord races, but they would bend against strong winds. Kayumalon was the country of brown-skinned Kayuman humans who settled here with the landing of the Maragtas kings. These same rulers saw it best to conquer the surrounding lands of their ever-expanding settlements, which included the lands of Tikbalang horse humanoids, the Asinari merfolk, the Dalaket tree folk, and the Asuwan undeads—the four non-human races that the Kayuman called the strangelords.

'Girl, did you hear me?' She heard the rumble of his footsteps, wooden feet on wooden floor, approaching her, gnarled tree-bark hands forcing her to turn away from the railings. 'Oh, it's you. You pale-faced Dayo all look alike!'

'Enough of that, Captain,' said her father, his tattoos hidden beneath layers of clothes, including the ones on his face. He steadied her with a protective hand.

There was a saying among the Kayuman, *'Nagbabalatkayo ang nagtatago ng balat'*—never trust a man who hides his skin—so her father pulled down his mask, exposing the black stripe tattoos on his face. It was barely a hint of the grander tattoos all over his body, but it seemed enough to put the captain in his place. 'We'll be out of your foliage soon enough.'

Yin suspected that her father hid his tattoos out of habit rather than any real need to hide them. In their previous homes, he used to put them on display while he worked on the seedfields to keep cool against the heat. The Dayo feared him, but the Kayuman and the strangelords saw the tattoos as a mark of a rank he had earned in a previous life.

'Good riddance to your lot! We'll be docking soon,' the captain said, returning to the helm and barking orders at his crew along the way.

'I told you to keep your head down,' her father muttered, putting the mask back on but leaving a strip of open space for his eyes.

Yin nodded, the movement helping her long hair hide her face. She gathered it on one side and held it there. 'I wasn't doing anything . . .'

She felt her father tense up next to her, as if he was burned by such a simple statement of fact. 'There are enough halflings on this island for you to blend in, but that doesn't mean you can be careless.'

She thought about what her father had said. It sounded like a promise, a guarantee that she could be safe here if she didn't do anything dumb, but she knew, like any Dayo intrinsically knew, that the Dayo were not citizens of this country, but vassals of it. Still, she allowed herself to think of the possibilities on this island. On the one hand, there would be more people who might accept her as she was. On the other, it could mean that this island was more prone to violence against Dayo, which unfortunately seemed to be the case for many seedplantations across the country.

'Nowhere is safe for Dayo, father. Why did you bring me here? This is Kayuman land. I'm more likely to get randomly killed by a Kayuman Red just because I'm pale-skinned.'

'Many things are lost just by hiding in plain sight.'

She shot him a judging look from the corner of her eye. 'You would sacrifice Dayo who looked like me to hide me?' She said, unable to hide the disdain in her tone.

Her father didn't answer, but it didn't matter. She knew his answer: He would have dozens of Dayo girls killed to protect Yin. She'd seen him do it before.

'This is disputed land between the three Kayuman Datus—Lakantabi, Lakanlupa, and Maragtas Isles,' her father said. 'If any of your pursuers tried to capture you here, the other two would see it as an advance on the territory and retaliate.'

*So we are being pursued by one of the Kayuman Datus?* Was the question she wanted to ask—and she almost did, out of habit. However, she tried to curb her curiosity because it was of no use. She knew she wouldn't be getting any answers. But the curiosity still lingered, building up inside her like an ember that was waiting to blaze into a raging fire at the slightest provocation.

'Why didn't we hide out here in the first place?'

He scoffed. 'I wouldn't even come here now if I had a choice.'

'Why?'

'Your mother was born here,' he said, his words reeking of grief and uttered with a tone of finality that warned Yin not to probe further. There was more to it than that, she knew. Whenever her father spoke of her mother, it was always tinged with a hint of melancholy, as if he'd lost her even before she had died.

By now the ship was low enough that she could see the people milling about the docks and the long stretch of the market street leading up to the town square. A blaze of red caught her eye. Pale skin, ginger hair, towering height, gorgeous, easy-going smile, the most beautiful Dayo she has ever seen in all the ten provinces of Kayumalon. She couldn't look away.

'How long will we live here?' She asked, hugging herself against the cold seawater breeze. For as long as she could remember, her family had never stayed longer than a year in one place. Not long enough to build even a semblance of a life, but long enough to learn how people reacted to strangers in their hometown.

It was generally the same. They would approach Yin with caution, then draw back in fear when they found out that her father was a former high-ranking Kayuman soldier. Some even made up stories about them, spinning tales wherein Yin and her father would always be chased out of their previous homes by outraged mobs. None of it was true though; at least that was what Yin thought. She was never sure, and her father never really told her about his old life.

She snapped out of her reverie when her father moved. He looked down at her with eyes that were softened by kindness, and she was taken aback by the sudden show of affection. Her father was not the kind of person who would open up to her about what he felt—not since before her mother's passing—and yet there it was, the telltale signs of a smile that was being given freely to her. 'Not any longer than necessary.'

Suddenly, the ship rocked as it splashed into the docks with a loud boom, catching her by surprise, making her unsteady on her own two feet and taking her far, far away from touching the sky.

# Chapter 2

## Kalem

*A Month Ago*

A vial uncorked with a sharp pop between shelves of books and scrolls of tattooed skin history. The seedshooter, the white iridescent liquid it contained, emptied through lips hungry for power. This liquid magic from the gods flowed like blood through Kalem Laya's veins but left stains skin-deep in its wake.

Kalem closed his eyes, feeling the magic course through his body, feeling it fill him. The liquid flowed down his throat, past his stomach, and into a metaphysical organ in the body more spiritual—more divine—than physical, where the magic was metabolized. Seven seeds, seven types of magic, all waiting for their turn to be summoned, all approximating the power of the Skyworld gods for just a few minutes: red for adrenaline, orange for muscle mass augmentation, yellow for pheromones, green for illusions and vision manipulation, blue for mood depressants and stimulants, indigo for healing and body regeneration, and violet for muscle relaxants that led to increased flexibility.

He crouched there, unmoving among the books and scrolls and the scent of ageing paper and dried skin. Still the magic permeated out of him, a mixed scent of ginger, alatilis, eucalyptus and brimstone. He was too small a vessel for the full might of the gods. Even small doses could not be stomached by him. He needed to use the magic before it had a chance to drain out of him.

He stood up, hood low over his dark hair, covering his tattooed face and neck. His long black tunic and trousers covered every other tattoo on his body; ink stains he'd had since he was a boy in his father's court, symbols and sigils of his family, of loyalties and politics and rank.

A man in his position was expected to put his tattooed brown skin on display, but he'd never been comfortable displaying ink he didn't earn. Save for the one tattoo on his chest, the upturned leaf with the pattern of veins and seeds—the symbol of germachemy. This tattoo he had earned by hard work and diligent study. It was next to House Laya's turtle sigil—Kalem's family sigil—the same sigil his Datu father used. Even in daylight, he kept it all hidden—a school mandate. Scholarship must remain neutral.

But tonight, he was no scholar. He was not a germachemist. Nor was he a Datu's son. He would be a thief in the night.

The old saying, *'Nagbabalatkayo ang nagtatago ng balat'*—never trust a man who hides his skin—echoed in the back of his mind in his father's voice. It seemed parts of him were always constantly at odds with one another.

He shook off the doubt and lit his veins blue, the scent of eucalyptus and mint wafted off his skin in a cloud of glittering blue mist. Blue was meant to ease moods, induce a sense of calm in the people who would catch a whiff of the magic. Enough of it, and they fell asleep. It felt wasteful lighting up blue merely to illuminate his way. He was alone in this section, but blue was the vein stain that faded the fastest of the seven.

An echo sounded into the night, like the murmur of a thousand people talking at the same time. Of course, no one else but Kalem could hear it. It came and went when he used seedmagic, leaving in its aftermath a chilling message.

Ignoring the voices, he walked out of his hiding spot, a dark corner of the Archive in the lower floors where most of the skin scrolls were kept. It was a restricted area of the Archive, one requiring special permission from the headmaster for access. Unfortunately, he was rarely on the headmaster's good side. He had to sneak in during the day, hide behind the farthest shelves, and wait until the archivists closed the library for the night.

He ran his hands over spines of books and rolled-up scrolls of skin history. He'd read most of these books, of course. He'd dedicated almost half his life to studying germachemy in Kolehiyo. Germachemy was the study of magic gleaned from 'seeds' purified and distilled to make seedshooters, the vials of magic, which give germachemists, or 'seedmages' powers, depending on the kind of seed the magician chose to metabolize. The ability to use seedmagic was a rare skill even among the Kayuman, inherited from ancestors who, if the legends were to be believed, were the descendants of gods. It was believed that those of the

Maragtas bloodlines, the bloodlines of the first settlers of Kayumalon, were the most likely to inherit the skill. He'd been studying here for ten years. He knew that whatever it was he was looking for, he wouldn't find it among the journals and skin scrolls of dead scholars, nobles and priests.

He took a random one out and read the title, *Tales from the Skyworld Realms*.

It figured. He'd picked out the one book meant for children in this collection of Kayumalon mythology. The seedgods did have a sense of humor.

He cracked the book open at a random chapter and read the title of the story there, 'The Great Skyworld Race'.

He'd studied a bit of germachemical anthropology in his research for arcane seedsickness cures—on a whim, of course. He needed a break from his usual laboratory work. This story began as a song children chanted while playing *tagu-taguan*, a game—where one child would seek out his friends who went into hiding—which could be traced back to the era of the exodus of kings. It was only put to paper—in this case, inked on the skin of Balensusa the Wise's reign, which was three to four centuries after the Kayuman conquests. But it was Balensusa's own brother, Patas the Eloquent, who had painstakingly recorded these stories. However, he had a proclivity to make things more dramatic than they actually were. So 'The Great Skyworld Race' turned into 'The Revolution of Gods', which spawned several other retellings, thus convoluting the story further.

But the basic gist was the same: moon gods raced each other across the sky trying to cross into Skyworld—the palace of gods—before the coming of the eternal night. In another version of the mythos of the seven moons, it was said that a dragon, the great Bakunawa, would one day rise from the ocean to eat the seven moons one by one and plunge the world in an eternal night that not even the Morningstar could subdue alone.

In some versions, Skyworld was the god broken into a thousand pieces, each with unique powers that they must use to try and reform the god before an unknown entity plunged the many realms into eternal darkness.

Another echo in his head, screeching this time like metal scraping on glass. Hard to ignore, though he's stopped trying to. The voices always came when he used seedmagic.

Sighing, he returned the book to its place on the shelf. He was stalling, the rational part of him could tell. But he wasn't nervous about sneaking into the headmaster's office several floors above this section of the Archive. At this point, magic, to him, felt like second skin, one that he could summon instinctively. He'd trusted the magic with his life on more than one occasion. 'The most brilliant germachemist of his generation', his mentor Master Makabago had once said about him.

No, he was afraid of what he would find—or wouldn't find. He'd been working on this study for years and all his research had led him to mythologies—dead-ends and cold trails. The headmaster's personal collection was his last hope. If it yielded nothing, he had wasted ten years of his life—years he could have spent with his dying father who was in the throes of seedsickness. All he wanted was to find the impossible cure to his father's impossible disease.

He drew in a deep breath—sure that if there were other people near him, they would have already fallen asleep from the waves of blue magic he'd sent outward—and stepped onto the window ledge. He was high enough that he could see over the two walls surrounding the school and separating the campus from the rest of the city. The inner wall housed lecture halls and laboratories, and the outer wall contained the dormitories.

The Alaala Archive was a stone tower with an abnormally enormous Balai-lamok tree, fed and mutated by magic within the tower, growing over it, its thick trunks and roots curling over the tower's body and reaching up to the sky with branches that were heavy with white flowers and green leaves. The tree was always in full bloom and raining white petals over the school grounds below, no doubt an effect of the inherent magic of the tower. After a century of growing, the tree itself had covered so much of the tower that it wasn't unusual to think that maybe the tower itself was built within the tree.

His veins switched from lighting blue to violet for flexibility, and he extended an arm upward, reaching up to the closest trunk above the window. He turned off the violet and let the recoil of his arm returning to its natural length lurch him upwards. He used the momentum to leap up to the next branch above, lighting red for agility and then violet again for flexibility in quick intervals—so that it seemed like he was using two seedmagics at the same time.

Seedmagic can only be used one at a time, and it took rigorous training to master the quick switches—a part of his education that his mentor had drilled into him so very diligently. He continued the process till he reached the trunk right below the window of the headmaster's chambers. There was only one way up to his room, or at least one way that a rational person would use—a spiral staircase along the inner wall of the archive that ended within the head archivist's chambers on the bottom floor.

Kalem's way was a . . . creative alternative.

The voices came again, as whispers this time, and Kalem pointedly ignored them, lest he lose concentration and fall to the ground below. His body would break, but he had enough indigo to repair him. At least he thought he had enough.

No use worrying about that now. His veins were lit violet as he extended both hands towards the window ledge and he paused to take in a breath, preparing to switch to red and then to green. He counted to ten but didn't wait for the last number to trigger the recoil, and went leaping up and landing on the ledge lightly, activating the green just in time to render himself practically invisible.

His shadow cut into the moonslight streaming through the window and onto the floor behind the headmaster's tan narra desk and chair. He slipped off the ledge and crouched in the shadows below the window.

Green interfered only with light that hit the eyes and the mage's body and not with the light itself. Hiding the shadows and the imprint cast by the mage's still-tangible body were the tricky parts. Those often gave away the mage, especially when drawing illusions outside of himself.

He looked up at the room from behind the desk and saw the headmaster's office from a new angle. Often, he stood on the other side of the desk, head bowed down, waiting for the headmaster to stop waxing poetic between scoldings. The room itself was conical shaped, capped with a high domed ceiling and divided by a mezzanine, part of which was the enclosed sleeping quarters where the headmaster should be sound asleep right then. Every inch of the walls was covered with shelves of books, save for the windows above and below the mezzanine floor. The large open window through which Kalem had entered the room was situated behind the desk, and even from there Kalem could see shelves stretched across the sleeping quarters, holding bottles, vials and jars of seedmagic formulas and common herbs.

Kalem turned off green, leaving his veins stained with the colour of the last magic he had used. It was quiet, not the eerie nighttime quiet of his home in Maylaya, but the kind of quiet made by a large, densely populated city like Castel, which never seemed to sleep.

Maylakanon may be the Maragtas kings' seat of power, but Castel was the city that ran the country. Here, the many lords and Datus and bannermen of Kayumalon gathered to decide the fate of their own regions and of the country, going so far as setting up embassies in the island city far from their own fiefdoms to maintain a solid presence and influence there.

He walked along the shelves under the mezzanine, eyes straining to read the titles on the spines by the moonslight coming in through the window. The Headmaster had a private collection of arcane seedmagic books that predated Maragtas the Conqueror's reign, books and resources that weren't even on display in the museum on the outer wall. He knew the maestro had many of them based on the many bibliographies that the headmaster enumerated in his own books in the general Archives.

Most of the books on the lower floor were general reference books on germachemy and biology, so he climbed the spiral staircase right next to the double doors and began to look through the titles on the mezzanine.

He timed the steps with the beating of his heart, which seemed to drown out every other sound in the room. At the top of the stairs, he realized that he was nervous, but that didn't stop him from walking onto the platform that lined the mezzanine and over to the big room, towards the bookshelves.

He'd waited so long to see these books. He'd patiently followed the rules, filled out forms, and sent handwritten requests. He had taken his time, but clearly there was no incentive in following the rules, so he had resorted to bribing the archivists to help him access these books in secret. He was caught when an Archive apprentice ratted him out to the head archivist. His punishment was taking classes for the practical applications of germachemy—extra combat training—for six months. He hated combat training and would have done away with it if his mentor had not mandated him to train every morning for the past ten years. He was stronger after those six months, sure, but also so very exhausted.

Now he had no time. He would be graduating next month—if the headmaster allowed it—and then he'd have to join his father in court. He had always pictured himself as a scholar, not a politician, but his father had more faith in him than he did in himself. He was, however, afraid that when he did join his father, he would have to give up everything he had worked for his entire life, everything he had found out about godvessel magic, and every hope of finding a cure for his father's seedsickness.

So, he had taken matters into his own hands and had come up here the hard way. Now, finally, the books were within his reach.

He stood on the walkway of the mezzanine, stopping before four bookshelves, each spanning the width of his outstretched arms. At the very top of each shelf were skin scrolls tattooed with black ink. At the bottom were faded leatherbound books with yellowing paper pages. Some of these books didn't even have titles on the spines, or at least they weren't visible to the naked eye. Many of the books in the restricted sections needed germachemical assistance to read the contents, which limited the number of people who could access them.

He took out, from a pocket within his cloak, a clear sphere the size of a marble with a small green mung bean seed inside and shook it, lighting the seed and turning it into a portable glow lamp. He raised the sphere up to the books and the titles written in old baybayin text materialized where the green light fell on them.

He did a quick scan of the books, and unsure if he'd read the titles right, did another scan, this time making sure he read each and every title clearly.

*The Rebels of Red Dawn, The Weight of Dusk, The Breath of War, The Eye of the Sky, The Edge of The Worlds, The Veins of Power, The Seeds of Conquest, The Revolution of Gods. The Rise of the Dragon . . .*

These were the complete set of Patas the Eloquent's retellings of the Skyworld mythologies, long thought to be lost to time and damage, plus the retellings these books later spawned.

He pulled out one book, flipped through the pages, scanning and barely understanding the text, and then cast it aside to move on to another book. He didn't need to understand the books completely. These were not the technical germachemical books he needed for his experiments and were not at all like instructional manuals that he could use in his study.

These were fiction. Nonsense fairytales. Mythological and religious dead-ends.

In his desperation, he cast aside the marble with its meagre light and lit his own veins green, pulling out book after book, carelessly throwing them aside after he'd scanned the inside pages. He did this till he had emptied out the shelves. He couldn't even get himself to care about the noise he was making, still in denial that all his effort to get here, to see these books, to study the magic, had been in vain. There *must* be something he could use here.

He looked up at the scrolls as his hopes of finding anything useful, anything at all that wasn't nonsense, slowly deserted him. Skin scrolls contained the story of men, their banners, symbols, House sigils, loyalties, politics, and rank, many of which were glorified—as if the ink would make the men seem bigger than they actually were in death. Manufactured glories. Iterations of stupid, nonsensical fairy tales.

Kalem reached for the scrolls anyway, knowing full well that he was even less likely to find anything useful there. He haphazardly unfurled skin scrolls on top of the mess he had already made, some rolling away and unraveling down the side of the railings and off the mezzanine. Imperial advisors, germachemists, Alagadan priests, and former headmasters of Kolehiyo. He read through them with the desperation of a man dying of thirst in the middle of the ocean.

The last scroll, Patas' skin itself, told the story of a life spent chasing stories, of places he'd visited, of people he'd met in his lifetime. Kalem let that fall to the side as he knelt before the shelves, his veins glowing green over the shadow his body made in front of him.

The seven moons were framed in the floor-to-ceiling window behind the tan narra desk. Their combined light cast an odd gleam into the room. Another light, coming from a blue glow lamp from the sleeping quarters, came forward along with the rustling of robes.

'Master Laya, have you lost your mind?' The headmaster screeched.

Kalem didn't bother to look up, his eyes still on the storyteller's scroll, eyes brimming with tears, the voices in his head shouting for attention. He didn't care. What could the headmaster do to him? Punish him with more combat training? Threaten him with expulsion?

It all seemed futile now, ridiculous even, considering what he had to face.

This was another dead-end, another failure. Perhaps he should have listened to his father and stopped wasting his life trying to chase a myth. His father has long accepted that he wouldn't live long and had tried to help Kalem make his peace with that.

But Kalem couldn't. Too much was at stake for him to give up so easily.

# Chapter 3

## Dakila

*Present Day*

Dakila's entire life was dictated by the gods. He was, by divine right, heir to the Kayumalon throne.

*If only he was born before his brother Dangal. If only he was his father's trueborn son.*

Stripped of his armor and princely garb, all his tattoos hidden, his usually loose long black hair tied in a neat knot behind his head, he knelt in a secluded conclave within the Alagad Temple's inner sanctum. It should annoy him that he was not alone. Back in Maylakanon, a conclave was always reserved for him—being the devout Alagadan that he was—but Castel was a promiscuous city; 'neutral' was the official word used in the parliament. It did not care for nobility enough to distinguish which ones were superior to the others.

He was a lord feigning humility. That was the role he was playing now.

Surely, Dakila was superior to the country-bumpkin noble from the far reaches of the ten kingdoms kneeling next to him in *his* conclave. There was enough space on the common floor for them, crowded as it was on this day, the Day of the Reaping.

The temple itself was a domed stone structure that opened at the top, where the ancient fire tree with red and orange flowers reached out its branches to the Skyworld. Around the hole were seven strategically placed lunette windows, each embellished with the symbols and colours of the moon it represented and framed on the days when the moons were visible in the sky. The positions of the lunettes were more than decorative. Depending on which lunette the Morningstar was visible through, one would be able to tell the time. Narrow rectangular windows were lined up in neat rows along the walls below the hole letting the noon light and summer wind flow into the space. At the base of the stone walls were several conclaves reserved for nobles. Devotees knelt in every space available on the multicoloured marble-tiled floor surrounding the giant tree. On regular days, the pattern of the seven moon gods on the floor glittered with the seven lights.

'Seven divine virtues. Seven divine sins. Seven spheres of light,' chanted the Alagadan priest in arcane dialect. He wore a patterned bahag, a thick loincloth that hung from a belt and fell to the knees, of seven colours, his brown skin a canvas of black tattoos, his curly black hair sleek with sweat and oil, an ornate dagger—black from blade to pommel—raised above his head. He'd been at it for hours. Chanting and dancing and circling the tree like an animal prowling the carcass of its hunter. The tree's base was hollow and the roots that stretched out on the exposed soil and under the marble floor created a space—a sort of nest—where an old, withered woman lay in a death-like sleep, clutching the totem of a tiger—a war god's spirit animal—to her chest. A small boy, who looked to be around five years old, was crying and kneeling before the woman. He was held down by his own father and mother who knelt on either side of him.

The country bumpkin spoke suddenly. 'Lots going on in our empire, eh?'

Dakila pressed his lips together but didn't react, didn't let a single strand of hair tremble. He resisted the urge to look at the man and betray how he felt. In all things, a man of his position must maintain a dignified demeanor. From the corner of his eye, however, he laid judgment on the bumpkin. The man had the sigil of a minor house on his chest, right under the sigil of the great House he served and letter markings of his rank. Based on the patterns of the sash over his sleeveless plain top and dark pants and the unmistakable smell of brine and seawater emanating from his skin, the bumpkin must be from the south—Maylaya or Maragtas Isles likely—though he wouldn't have been surprised if he was from some place more exotic like Olimawi or Asinar. Typical of the southerners to wear their colours at a Temple gathering—costumey, showy, ostentatious—but it irked him that he looked like the inferior noble between them.

The bumpkin went on, 'Invaders in the north. Dayo rebellion in the south. Political instability in the east. Plague on yellow seeds. And the council is fighting internally about everything. Nothing gets done. This vote to defend our borders against invaders shouldn't even be a question. Everything's a political issue nowadays. How do they even talk to each other?

What has happened to our country? Us simple folk down south just want to work our keep, you know? Three meals a day—'

Dakila felt the muscle above his brow twitch. Still, he didn't turn to acknowledge the man.

The scar-faced stranger was right. There was so much going on at the top. With the Payapas gone, murdered by scrupulous methods just a few months ago, Congress had become an arena of political standoffs between major and minor Houses and among Datus with beef against the ruling House. The Payapas had served as the country's neutral good, siding with neither strangelords nor Kayuman. Be it conservatives or liberals, monarchists or abolitionists, they somehow pleased everyone at Congress except one—the one person who was most threatened by the Payapa's influence. Everyone knew who orchestrated it, but no one would dare air that fact out in the open and risk civil war.

The Alagadan droned on, waving the black dagger about as he made slow dances around the tree. Forty-nine circles in total, seven for each cycle of the moon spheres. Dakila had already lost count of how many he'd done thanks to the bumpkin, who was still talking.

'Now, I hear the crown prince has a Dayo princess alive and alone somewhere far away—'

Dakila's ears quivered at that one, and he faced the bumpkin to see that the man wasn't even looking at him. He seemed to be talking to himself, the way senile elders did when they were alone. The man wasn't even old but the burn scar on his face, so deformed that his right eye was perpetually squinting, added years to the man's appearance—he could have been Dakila's age.

'—It's likely from the queen's side of the family. The king's sister, Datu Patas' wife? She made it worse for the family bloodline. But House Laya's bloodline has always been cursed, being Maragtas descendants themselves. It's the inbreeding, I tell you. Maragtas descendants marrying each other. The Maylaya Datu himself, like the Maylakanon king, is already sick and dying, too—' The bumpkin tsk-ed, taking himself too seriously. 'So much bad luck at the top. Datu Duma likely passed the curse to his sons, as well. The older one is drinking himself to seedsickness. And the other, well, let's just say he can't produce heirs with the partners he's choosing. Rumor has it the second one's the queen's bastard, too. Neither, surely, are fit to lead the charge of war against the invaders.'

Dakila's hand went reflexively to his belt only to find that his sword or dagger wasn't there. The scarred man didn't seem fazed by his sudden movement, but he turned to look at Dakila anyway.

A strange, confused silence settled on the man, the kind that fell on a martyr suddenly forced to kneel in front of a chopping block. The sharp, murderous look in Dakila's eyes flashed for a second, but he reined it in, remembering where he was and which character he was playing now.

'You know what to do,' he said, turning away sharply just as the bumpkin scrambled to find the farthest spot from him possible, under the red moon's lunette window. The sky outside had begun to drift into the afternoon as the ritual went on.

He turned his attention back to the Alagadan, who was moving significantly slower now around the tree, the dagger barely raised higher than his shoulder. He would be done soon.

For a quick second, he thought the bumpkin didn't actually know that he was talking to Dakila Maylakan, Commander of the Kalasag Cavalry, second son of Duma, the fourteenth King of Kayumalon. He shrugged the thought off, remembering that he was playing a character.

If he were next in line, he'd make sure every corner of this country knew the king's face. He'd make sure the country feared and revered the king's name.

But he wasn't next in line. His brother Dangal was, and he left Maylakanon a month ago presumably to drink, shoot seeds, and streetwalker around on this island city and had not been seen since. Of course, his father had sent Dakila to find Dangal and make sure he was at the Congressional vote a week from today.

A dark, malicious part of him stirred and rattled the cage in his heart, the one that held back every bad thought he'd had about his father, the one that woke up the grief he felt for the death of his mother. *He* was the good son. *He* was the diligent son. *He* was the obedient son. *He* was the perfect son.

His father couldn't even look him in the eye.

Dangal went out of his way to anger their father, and Dakila cleaned up the mess—tavern brawls, uncontrollable gambling, an illegitimate child, exorbitant debts, and murder. He did all those with nary a complaint to his father or his brother. He did it all quietly as if it never really happened.

The Alagadan stopped in front of the sleeping woman. The chanting changed. *'Dirigmaaaaaaa!'* He yelled, a summoning, an entreaty to a divine entity. His voice echoed within the dome, rustling flowers off their branches. Red and orange petals rained over the devotees, who called the crimson god by his ancient name, *'Dirigmaaaaaaa!'*

Dakila chimed in, barely understanding the word in his mouth, eager for the next part.

The Alagadan took the boy from his parents and led him to the sleeping woman. He whispered into the boy's ear and then placed the dagger in his palm. The boy trembled and then cried.

The boy turned to his parents, who were duty-bound by religion to stay where they were, calling the war god's name with the rest of the crowd. They were no longer his parents. He was no longer just a boy. The boy, like the woman, was chosen, born to be offered to the gods.

From the next moment, that boy would be a vessel of the gods for the rest of his life. It was rare that the Alagadan would choose someone so young for this. But in times like these, war gods demanded an exorbitant price.

The Alagadan prodded the boy forward, the blade awkward in his grip, his hand shaking as he raised it over the old woman's chest. The dagger hovered over her, trembling, but did not descend. The call for the god rose and rose and rose till it reached the crescendo, the scream of a thousand voices making the air vibrate with energy that sent currents under Dakila's skin. He felt a shiver work its way up from the base of his torso.

Dakila's heart pounded in his chest, his breath ragged as he called the war god's name with the rest of the supplicants, *'Dirigmaaaa! Dirigmaaaa! Dirigmaaaa!'* Eyes on the tip of the blade that now rested on withered, dying brown flesh. Hands sweaty with anticipation.

When the boy did not move still, the Alagadan knelt next to him, whispered into his ear, and pressed the boy's forearms down, lowering the dagger into the old woman's chest, piercing through skin and sternum, and cleaving her heart open. The boy moved to let go of the knife, but the priest would not allow him, screaming at the top of his lungs, 'Seven divine virtues. Seven divine sins. Seven spheres of light. Red blood riding across the sky. First in battle, last to die. *Dirigma*, your people beckon, awaken when the time for war is nigh.' He urged his followers to repeat the words.

Blood spurted out of the woman's chest, splashing on the boy's hands and face, her grip on the totem loosened. The Alagadan held the boy's hand to the blade, even after the child had fainted from crying.

The chanting slowed and then dissipated, but it stopped only when the priest picked the boy up and called for younger acolytes to take the old woman's body away. He laid the boy in the hollow where the woman had been and placed the totem in his small hands. When the time came, the boy's dead body would follow the same fate as the withered woman. Panting, the Alagadan raised both hands over the boy in prayer then stood to face the audience, solemnly and with the depth of a soldier who'd been saved from a losing battle by the cavalry.

'The old god has passed. A new god is born.'

Dakila was panting as he repeated the words, mulling over what this meant. His eyes fell to the offending bumpkin across the hall, his forehead on the floor, hands stretched out, palms up in supplication—a show like no other.

Dakila drew in a deep, exhilarating breath as he dipped his head to the floor, then exhaled as he stood and left the temple. He was going to find his brother and clean up his mess once and for all.

# Chapter 4

## Yin

Masalanta Island was hardly a small town, especially when compared to the plantation towns Yin had lived in before. It was not big enough to be a city like the great metropolises of Maylakanon or Maylaya, but it was bigger than the Castel university town.

The people here knew of each other and not each other, and barely paid any notice to the newcomers coming in from the docks. It was easy to blend in, but that was only good for people who weren't planning on staying long on the island. The challenge was settling in, letting people get to know them and working to get them to accept newcomers like Yin and her father.

They'd been here two weeks, and the section of the island they lived in was primarily occupied by Kayuman families who married the Dayo workers.

It wasn't exactly forbidden for Kayuman to marry outside of their people, but there were certainly consequences to it.

Marriage to a Dayo meant that their contract of ownership had been officially bought by their Kayuman partners. It didn't mean freedom, but there was an unspoken understanding that they had a slightly more elevated rank than the other Dayo. The freedom only applied to their halfling children, but it was a tenuous freedom at best. Pure Kayuman still discriminated against their paler-skinned fellowmen.

The Kayuman who married a Dayo, on the other hand, got a tattoo marking them as tolerants—or, in the more derogatory version, blood defilers. It was a tree cleaved into two, down to the base. Most tolerants put their marriage tattoos on their ring fingers, over the vein that went straight to the heart, but her father had a different set of tattoos on his chest and fingers, from a life as a soldier when he was young, blacked out with ink to hide which sigils he once swore fealty to. In fact, her father's ring finger had been blacked out where a marriage tattoo might have been. It had been that way for as long as she could remember. Meanwhile, her mother's marriage brand—the Dayo who marry Kayuman were branded with the same mark using hot irons—was carved out, leaving a nasty scar around it.

Most of the Kayuman living on this side of the island had these ink and scar markings, and she spent the first few days of living on the island counting them until she just gave up and concluded that there were far too many scarred but free people here.

Her father had taken on a foreman's job at one of the haciendas in the valley. It was one of the biggest yellow seedplantations in the country—which put them at the very top of the social ladder. It was akin to being the high priest's child during the temple worship ceremonies. It was lonely being the chief foreman's daughter in a plantation.

So, on the first days here, she decided that she would try to make friends, set down roots, and make a life here. She heard about the Dayo her age, many of them halflings who worked the fields with their parents, gathering at a secluded beach at night after work to rest and unwind and do whatever it was that young Dayo did in their free time. Yin never stayed long enough in a city to find out, and she was determined to find out now; now that they can stay for as long as they want.

That was when she saw the boy again. He was surrounded by people, his friends, she supposed, laughing at whatever joke he had told them. He noticed her immediately when she walked onto the beach in a wraparound dress that swayed in the ocean breeze, and, unused to attention, Yin didn't know how to react. She smiled at him sheepishly before averting her eyes and slouching in an effort to look small. For as long as she could remember, her father had warned her against drawing unwanted attention and reminded her, time and time again, to stay out of the spotlight. She never understood why, and for the life of her, she couldn't understand why she should when it felt good to be noticed by this beautiful boy.

Without wasting another second he walked away from his friends sitting around the bonfire and approached her.

'You know, I haven't seen you around before,' he told her, his voice smooth as the sea on a clear summer's day.

'I'm new here,' she said, feeling smaller under his towering height. He smelled like raw yellow seeds mixed with saltwater and a scent that seemed to particularly belonged to him. She couldn't help but lean in slightly, just for another whiff. 'I've only been here a few days.'

'Where have you been all my life?' He said, jokingly. 'No wonder the sun seemed brighter the last few days. Where were you before this?'

'I came from an indigo plantation in Maylaya,' she answered naively, sensing that that wasn't the answer he had wanted. He laughed because she was silly, and he was silly, and this was all new to her. The wind blew, the sound passing through like laughter, and it made strands of her hair dance around her face. As if on impulse, he tucked her loose hair behind her ear, his fingertips grazing her cheek. He did this like he had meant to touch her subtly and it made her skin prickle with titillating electricity. She couldn't help giggling. She didn't even know she could giggle like that.

'I grew up on this island.' He said, his hand sliding down her arm. 'I'll give you a tour if you want.'

'I would like that,' she said airily, pretending like her breath had not just been sucker-punched out of her.

'What's your name?' He asked, his hand settling in her hand, holding it between them.

'Yin,' she answered, not bothering to add a last name. Dayo took the name of the island or province they were born in, but Yin had been changing last names all her life and none had stuck long enough for it to become habitual to use. She let him deduce her last name.

'I'm Tiyago Masalanta,' he answered, weaving his fingers through hers and leading her to the bonfire. 'Come meet my friends.'

He sat her down next to the spot he occupied earlier, in the middle of the crowd of his Dayo friends, and introduced her to them as 'Yin Maylaya'. Then he introduced each of his friends to her one by one. There were so many names and faces that she knew couldn't possibly remember them all. He didn't let go of her hand the entire time.

One skinny girl though, with green eyes and yellow hair, stared sharply at her with a smile that made Yin's skin crawl. She sat up from the man she had been leaning against, his arm around her waist loosening its hold on her.

'Who's the new girl, Tiyago?' She spoke to him in a tone used by those who shared a deep secret, the kind that kept outsiders like Yin out.

'She's Yin from Maylaya, Rejeena,' Tiyago said, looking at Yin like he was expecting her to explain herself.

'I came here just a few days ago,' Yin said, her palms sweating, slouching again and tucking her legs under her to make her look small again. A new understanding came to her. She liked Tiyago's attention, but an audience was a different matter. 'You are Rejeena? Where are you from?'

Rejeena looked to her friends, grinning and flicking her brows up and down like she was telling them a joke with her eyes. Suddenly, they all laughed. 'Oh, don't laugh *at* her. She's one of those.'

Yin tilted her head, brows furrowed, and looked at Tiyago questioningly. 'One of what?'

He pulled his hand from hers and scratched the back of his neck, glaring at Rejeena. 'Rejeena, be nice.'

'What? It's true—'

'Rejeena, I'm warning you . . .' Tiyago threatened, practically growling.

'Mudveined. White on the outside, mud on the inside,' Rejeena finished before a sudden clap echoed through the night, quieting the entire place. Even the sound of the waves lapping the shore was drowned out by the tense silence.

Tiyago had slapped Rejeena, who looked stunned beyond belief. Recovering, she got up and glared at Tiyago with tears in her eyes, and then gave Yin a look that clearly said, 'You'll pay for this,' before running back into the village. The guy she had been leaning on ran after her, cursing at Tiyago before he got far.

'Ignore her,' Tiyago said.

'Yeah! It's not the first time Rejeena—' one of his friends began saying, but was cut off when Tiyago gave him a look.

'What?' Yin asked, looking at each person sitting with them.

'Rejeena and I . . . We were . . .' Tiyago began to explain, grabbing a bottle of yellow wine from the sandy ground. 'Anyway, she's dating—' he mentioned a name that for the life of her she wouldn't remember if he hadn't pointed at the guy who chased Rejeena. 'It doesn't matter. We broke up months ago.' He took a swig from the bottle, which his friends seemed to take as a sign to continue with their own conversation and leave him alone with Yin. 'You want some?' He offered the bottle to her, practically forcing it into her hands.

'What is it?' She asked, sniffing the mouth of the bottle. It was sweet, like alatiris and mangoes, but with a sharp tang that reminded her of burning wood.

'It's Charmer's wine, made from boiled residue of yellow seedmagic,' he said, pushing up the mouth of the bottle to her lips. 'Try it. You'll feel better afterwards.'

'Seedmagic?' She pulled the bottle away, staring at it in the moonslight. 'Aren't Dayo forbidden from consuming seeds?'

'The seedshooters, yes. These are made from boiled discarded seedhusks. Barely any magic in there.'

She glanced between Tiyago and the bottle, reluctant to do as he insisted. She had a bad feeling about this. Her father forbade her from drinking seedshooters, but this was seedwine; it had to be different, didn't it?

'It's okay if you don't want to. I'll walk you home,' Tiyago said, beginning to stand up.

'No,' she said, pressing the bottle's mouth to her lips and tilting it upwards. The first drop was an explosion of sweet nectar on her tongue. It was a small dose, barely a dose, but her mind wavered, a voice speaking in tongues in her mind, her veins thrumming wildly under her skin. She pulled the bottle away, spilling some of it on the sand. The voices faded almost immediately, as if they hadn't spoken at all. Tiyago stared at her, flabbergasted, then at the spilled wine, and she realized her mistake. 'Sorry, let me try again . . .'

But before she could, an angry, gravelly voice called to her. 'Yin, what are you doing here? I told you to stay home!' Her father, with his tattoos on full display in the bright night, came stomping towards Yin, who scrambled up to her feet to run to him before he came any closer to their group.

'I wasn't doing anything, father,' Yin said, hands raised as if to stop him from marching further toward the other Dayo, who were beginning to scamper away.

'Go home, *mga alipin*!'[1] He said, stopping right in front of Yin and pointing his whip at Tiyago and his friends. 'It's lashing for your lot in the morning!'

The other Dayo—including Tiyago—who hadn't already fled after seeing her father proceeded to escape. Tiyago,

---

[1] 'Alipin' is an noun in the Filipino dialect, Tagalog, used to refer to those of lower social classes

however, took one last peek at Yin over his shoulder as he ran. But what she saw in his face stopped her cold. There was a patchwork of confusion and horror on his face as he realized who Yin really was. He'd uncovered Yin's greatest lie—that she was one of *them.*

Her father dragged her back home that night and told her off for being careless and impulsive. He then forbade her from going out at night again with the other Dayo her age, but it was just as well. The Dayo wouldn't let her join them again. She tried sneaking out again a week later, but they didn't return to that spot on the beach. She had ruined that for them, and she doubted she would get another chance with Tiyago.

# Chapter 5

## Dakila

*Eighteen Years Ago*

Dakila was in trouble. Again.

The Dayo servants had been saying, *'May tenga ang lupa may pakpak ang balita'* over and over in the same breath while they'd been speaking about his older brother Dangal. 'The young prince who's fallen off his pedestal', they called him. 'The Kayuman boy who was pale underneath', they whispered amongst each other behind his back. 'The boy who had the moons in the palm of his hand and star crowns atop his dark-haired head and endless night inked on his Kayuman skin'.

His nursemaid Caritas told him to think nothing of the talk between servants and lesser men. They didn't matter anyway. What mattered was what they both thought of Dangal. She always said it with such sadness in her eyes, like she thought it was her fault all along. But how could it be her fault? She was only Dayo after all, paler than any other Dayo servant in the Maylakanon Palace. His father always said never to trust a man who hid his skin, but he never said what to do with the Dayo who didn't hide their pale skin—clear of ink. His father beat them, sent them away, ordered them around and summoned them to his chambers, but otherwise ignored them and their glaringly white skin.

That was why he ignored Caritas when she said not to wander around the parts of the palace he wasn't allowed to wander to.

Nevertheless, today, he was the one in trouble. He went about the palace searching for the plot of earth that had ears and wings and that had been talking ill about his brother. He searched the garden and its tree-lined lanes, which were heavy with the fruits of summer. He searched the inner courtyards for vines growing between gaps in the palace walls. He searched the rows of fragrant herbs growing wildly in pots on kitchen counters. He even searched every guest room where there were pots of citronella to ward off the mosquitoes. He went so far as running along the banks of the Arimoanga river, his feet and gilded sandals leaving muddy prints in the wet dirt until Caritas came running after him.

How he found himself in Maragtas Gallery, the archive of the royal family skins splayed out and displayed within conclaves in the walls, he could not remember. But the small muddy handprints on the tattooed skin-history that had been pulled off from its display and spread out on the floor like common leather were definitely his. He suddenly remembered seeing his brother talking to these musty, human-shaped skins and thought maybe these things had the ears he'd been looking for.

They didn't.

He had rubbed his tunic on the mud stain across the chest, harder and harder as the stains spread across the skin, ruining the fine leather and smudging the clean lines of ink. He had pulled away when he'd managed to tear a hole across the chest, and only then had he realized that he'd been crying the entire time.

'Dakila?' A voice called from the doorway of the hall, the large double doors swinging open gently to reveal Dangal in his Kolehiyo uniform, a black-and-white robe over black slacks and closed sandals. He cut a striking figure—so tall and strong and so very himself. 'What are you doing?'

Dakila backed away from his older brother, covering the ruined skin with his small body. 'Don't tell father, *kuya.*'

But there was no use hiding. He was simply too small to hide anything, too small to clean up after himself, too small to do anything other than cry. So he cried.

His brother crouched till he was eye-level with Dakila, leaning slightly to the side to see what he was hiding, and then sighed. 'Come on. Let's get you cleaned up. Caritas has been looking for you all over the palace.' He took his brother in his arms and carried him out the hall, giving orders to an aide waiting outside to clean up the mess Dakila had left in there.

Dakila buried his face in the crook of his brother's neck, still crying, still trembling with fear, still a child too small to understand that there were more important troubles than ruined skin history.

'Do you know whose skin that was, Kila?' His brother asked.

'Who?' Dakila asked into his brother's neck.

'That was our great, great, great, great, great, great, greeeeeeat grandfather, Maragtas the Peaceful,' Dangal said, laughing and making his shoulder shake against Dakila's cheek.

Dakila pulled back so he was looking at his brother's face. 'That's a lot of greats,' he said, giggling.

'Well, he's really old. He was the greatest king of Kayumalon, you know. He ended the wars, laid the groundwork for our economy, and built roads, bridges, and transportation lines between the ten balangays. He brought all the smartest and most talented people from all over the country to Castel to study and invent all sorts of machines and magic. It's because of him we don't go hungry during the dry seasons or homeless during the wet.'

Dakila buried his face back into the comfort of his brother's neck again. 'I ruined his skin . . .' he mumbled, against Dangal's skin.

'The skin doesn't matter more than the man, Dakila. The work he did during his time, the way he lived, the things he left behind, we see pieces of him everywhere, every day. We may lose the skin, but we don't lose that life's work.'

'You read that in a book again, Dangal?' Caritas said, walking up to them both. Dakila marvelled at how she seemed to appear out of nowhere, wearing a wide smile.

'As a matter of fact, Caritas,' Dangal answered, shifting Dakila to his other shoulder so he could look at her. 'This one's been in a lot of trouble while I was away, hasn't he?'

Dakila glared at him, but smiled when Caritas said, 'Not as much as you think. Your brother's been good all year.' She paused, offering to take the boy from his arms, but Dangal declined. 'You're home early from Kolehiyo,' she said, more a question than a statement, as they climbed the stairs going to the nursery.

'Being the king's son has *some* benefits.' Dangal grinned. 'How is my mother?'

Caritas shook her head. 'Some days, she's fine and up, finding work around the palace. Other days, she stays in bed, whispering to an empty room.'

The smile on Dangal's face fell, but he did not ask any more. Dakila watched the two talk about their year apart. About how Dangal had done during combat training. About how Caritas had found a secret thicket of guava trees further down the river. About how Caritas only had to wait two more years until Dangal finished Kolehiyo and would then stay at home for good.

It was a curious conversation. A Dayo servant and a Kayuman prince talking like old friends, and a part of Dakila told him that his father would disapprove of this.

*'May tenga ang lupa, may pakpak ang balita.'*

*Words have wings and the ground has ears.*

Dakila looked at his own muddy palms and then at the Dayo and the Kayuman, thinking he must have brought the earth with him.

# Chapter 6

## Yin

Yin didn't feel like she had truly settled into this new home. It wasn't for lack of trying. It seemed her father was determined to keep everyone away from Yin, and then there were those who avoided her for no reason other than hating her father for being their Kayuman master. Now, they glared daggers at her whenever they passed her on the street during their sojourn on market days.

The only person who didn't treat her like a walking bomb was Galenya, the aging albularyo and skyreader, mostly regarded by the other Dayo as deranged and unhinged until they needed her to treat their ailments. Yin chalked it up to Galenya's fading eyesight. Galenya said she simply attracted the most special human beings.

The first time she met the old healer, Yin was buying medicine for her monthly cramps, and the old woman grabbed her by the chin, read her face, stared for a good long time into her eyes until the word discomfort wasn't an adequate descriptor of what Yin felt about this invasion of personal space, and said, rather cryptically, 'I sense a power in you. Your destiny is bigger than yourself.'

'I don't understand,' Yin said as the woman pulled away and procured the herbs Yin needed from the shelves inside the crooked house on the edge of this section's village before Yin had even asked her to. It was as if the last few seconds hadn't happened at all.

'You regular ha? No, I'll give you more,' the old woman said, scooping up more leaves into a pouch and then handing it to Yin, her rough, wizened hands grazing against the young girl's smoother ones. 'Ah, you're Dayo who doesn't work in the fields. You need a job?'

Before Yin could answer, the woman grabbed a woven bag hanging by the door and handed it to her. It was surprising how the woman could find where Yin was in the room with her poor eyesight.

'You collect herbs for me in the mountain,' she said, sitting back down in front of the fire pit in the middle of her small house, over which a clay pot was coming to a boil. She threw several slivers of ginger into it. 'And ginger. Mangoes, too, if you can find them. You come back here for ginger tea.'

'I . . .'

'What? You don't know your herbs?'

'I do.'

'Then what are you waiting for? You're burning morningstarlight. No good up the mountain when redstar chases away the day.'

And three months later, that was how she came to spend her mornings gleaning and grazing in the mountains after her father had left for work. Upon her return, Galenya would sit her down and brew her ginger tea, which Yin sipped with delight until it was time for her father to return home.

Galenya also took patients in her home, reserving her bed for treatments that required healing beyond herbs. When there were such patients, Galenya—in her usual way of pretending that Yin's help was assured instead of assumed—would order Yin around, asking her to boil towels, wash tools, grind up herbs, and even clean and stitch wounds. There were some Kayuman patients, but most were Dayo labourers who came to seek aid after accidents on the field—or in a few rare cases, after a punishment.

'Galenya, how long have you done this?' Yin asked as she sorted herbs on the shelves. She had just returned from gleaning fresh herbs and fruit from the mountains for the old woman. It was a particularly busy day, which was always the case when the Reds—the colloquial word for the Kalasag soldiers coming from the capital—swarmed the island. 'Healing people, I mean.'

'Pretty long,' Galenya said as she handed off a fresh pouch of herbs to a Dayo with a big purple bruise on his face and a popped lip, and sent him on his way. She joined Yin at the shelves and helped her sort her finds. 'My father was an albularyo. My mother, a seedhealer.'

A handful of belladonna midway into a jar, Yin stopped to ask, 'Your mother was Kayuman?'

Galenya grabbed the belladonna from Yin's hand, tied a string around it, and hung it with the many others dangling from her ceiling. 'How do you think I get away with not working the fields like full Dayo?'

Yin shrugged. 'I figured healing was your job and you somehow talked your way out of hard labour.'

The old woman cackled. 'That I have!'

Yin sighted another patient shadowing Galenya's door, a Kayuman soldier, one of the nicer, more superstitious ones. The Kayuman, as a whole, were strangely superstitious. They didn't worship one monolithic deity but rather the pieces of gods that they believed were imbued in all things. It wasn't unusual for a Kayuman to ask skyreaders like Galenya to read their fortunes for them.

Galenya led the soldier to sit in front of the pot of boiling water. Yin was quick to take out the small box in the back of Galenya's closet and put it in the old woman's outstretched hand. Yin went back to the shelf to continue storing the herbs, all the while listening in on the conversation and stealing glances at the metal sphere Galenya had taken out of the box.

'You're infantry. Just one year into your enlistment. Loyalties to Lakantabi,' Galenya rattled off, looking over the soldier's tattoos along his arms and face; his uniform, a red vest and slacks held down by leather accessories, a black patterned scarf tied around his forehead to hold down his hair, and a sword lain across his lap. The soldier didn't look impressed. After all, these weren't actual predictions, but Galenya was fishing for more details. 'Born in the red moon month?'

The soldier confirmed all of it. 'Closer to the yellow moon, but not all the way, *Manang*.'[2]

Galenya nodded, then raised the metal sphere, making adjustments to the mechanisms following the symbols—

---

[2] In Ilocano, a dialect of the Filipino language, a term of respect given to an older woman, usually an older sister

traditional letters—etched on the surface. 'You were sent here to retrieve a symbol of power,' Galenya said, staring at the sphere and yet not really looking at it, as if she were watching a scene in the space between her eyes and the sphere. The sphere thrummed and vibrated in her hand, the mechanism spinning round and round, the surface shifting like melted alloy, a light, green and red and yellow and more auspiciously, violet, glowing from the inside. 'But it is power that ends all.' From here, she raised her gaze toward the soldier, looking increasingly frightened by the second. She leaned forward, her head practically hovering above the boiling pot, the steam rising around her, the heat bending the air all over, and suddenly the fire underneath blazed. 'Go! Go! Go now or suffer the gods' wrath, terrible as the dawn, sure as the wind.' The soldier scrambled up to his feet, almost dropping his sword, throwing coins on the ground, and running out the door without so much as a word of thanks.

The fire settled and Galenya blinked once, twice, and then a third time as if she had just woken up from a dream. Her hand to her throat, the other hand holding in a death-like grip the sphere that had settled back into her palm. She raised it up for Yin to take it, who then put it back in the box stored in the back of the closet.

'That sure scared him off,' Galenya said, ladling the ginger brew from the boiling pot into a clay cup. 'These Kayuman scare too easily.'

'You've been making a lot of predictions like that lately, Galenya,' Yin said, joining her in front of the fire. 'Always something about the wind and always only about the Kayuman. For the Dayo, the predictions have only been about breaking chains. Is it all true?'

'Child, these people don't always need divinations to know what they should do. Sometimes, they just need someone to say what they need to hear.'

'So, you told them what they needed to hear?'

Galenya turned her clouded eyes toward Yin, seeing and unseeing, but didn't answer.

'You gave me a prediction, too, when we first met. Did you just say it so you could make me work for you for free?'

Galenya laughed out loud. 'Divinations do have their uses.'

'That's not at all comforting, Galenya!'

'Ay, don't believe skyreaders. The sky changes at midnight all the time. We see what we want to see. We interpret the future we want to have.'

'That doesn't answer my question.'

'That's because you're not asking the right ones.'

'Okay, are skyreadings true?'

Galenya drank from her cup. 'As true as the gods walking among us.'

'So . . . not true?'

'And you know that for sure?'

'You don't believe in gods, Galenya. You believe in divine magic.'

'Smart girl,' Galenya answered like she had answered Yin's most burning questions—which she didn't, but Yin had learned not to push it. What was simple to Galenya always somehow became clearer to Yin later. Like that time Galenya had told her to collect as much makabuhay plant as she could days before a harvest festival. Yin bombarded her with questions as to why, but Galenya didn't answer. It turned out that more women came to Galenya's place after the festival, and looking at them and their swollen bellies was enough explanation for Yin. Though like the makabuhay incident, the explanations usually came at the most unexpected and inconvenient times.

'I don't understand why you still try to read the sky.'

'Money, child. You think a Kayuman household would hire the likes of me into their household?'

'Why did you learn skyreading anyway?'

'I didn't. It came naturally. Probably from the seedmagic inherited from my mother's side.' Galenya flicked her head toward the closet where Yin had stored the sphere. 'She gave me that, the astrolabe, which accurately predicts the position of the skies, past, present, and future. Then I read the symbols from there—' Galenya trailed off, listening for sounds from the doorway and sniffing the air. She put her cup down, stood up, and closed her eyelids, her head tilted toward the door. Yin watched in silence, waiting, until the old woman walked to the bed and began arranging the pillows and linen on it. 'I smell blood again.'

Yin turned to look at the door just in time to see a teenager with red hair be brought into the crooked house, held upright by a taller man. 'Galenya, help us, please."

'Tiyago?' Yin felt the blood drain out of her face.

Galenya directed him to the bed where he lay the younger man down, his lacerated back exposed through his shredded, bloody shirt. Tiyago watched Galenya look over the lashings, then scanned the room. He almost startled back when he saw Yin there, holding clean cloth to her chest, which she had intended to hand Galenya when she asked for it. She did and Yin put the cloth in the old woman's raised hand without another word.

'What happened?' Yin dared to ask Tiyago, who had had his jaw clenched the entire time Galenya cleaned the younger man's wounds.

'Reds,' Tiyago said without looking at Yin. 'More of them docked just this morning.'

'Why?'

'They found my brother and his friends smoking seedhusks. He let himself get caught so his friends could escape,' Tiyago said. 'The Kayuman don't even use the seedhusks to make their shooters.' He turned to her this time, unable to look at his brother as he squirmed in pain. 'The Kayuman king feels threatened. That's the only explanation I could think of for why there are more Reds here.'

'Why?' Yin asked before she could think about it.

'Masalanta is the biggest seedplantation in the entire country, Yin.' He folded his arms across his chest. 'Magic is power . . .' He mumbled to himself more, and Yin could only catch hints of what he was saying. 'They're weak . . . need us . . . not enough defence . . .'

Yin wasn't sure she understood what he meant, but she thought nothing more of it as Galenya called her over to get oregano to disinfect the wounds.

* * *

Later that night, her father returned home, agitated. He had locked the door and closed all the windows before settling in front of the fire where Yin cooked fish sinigang and white rice.

'The Dayo that the Reds caught today, you know them?' He asked as he took out a knife and a small vial containing thick indigo that glowed against the orange fire under the pots.

'Yes—' She flinched when her father glared at her, mouth pursed with words that were waiting to be spoken, pausing to allow her to explain herself. 'But only after his older brother, Tiyago, brought him to Galenya's house to heal, Father.'

'Did the Reds see you?'

'They probably did, but only the ones who came to Galenya's house for skyreading.'

His jaw clenched. 'They recognized you?'

'I think so. Reds come to Galenya all the time for skyreadings,' Yin answered, but she somehow got the impression that that wasn't the answer he wanted. 'I'm the healer's apprentice.'

That seemed to calm him, but she could still sense the tension. 'You learned how to clean a wound?'

Yin nodded, but she didn't like where this was going as he picked up the knife.

'Good,' he said. 'Get me a bowl of water.'

Yin did as she was told and set the bowl on the floor in front of him, wary of the knife her father held. He waved for her to step away. She reluctantly followed before he looked at his reflection in the water and sliced the first layer of tattooed skin on his cheek.

'Father!' Yin yelled, appalled, attempting to stop him, but he raised a hand.

'This is for your own good.'

'I don't understand.'

'You're the healer's apprentice. You should know what to do.'

And she did. Within seconds, she had clean cloth and oregano ready to clean the wound. When he was done, he growled, 'Shooter! Open it!'

With trembling hands, Yin popped the cork off the bottle, spilling a bit into her fingers. A buzzing came to her ears, muffled voices speaking in tongues, which she blamed on the adrenaline and utter shock of what her father had done. He grabbed the bottle from her and drained the contents into his mouth. His veins glowed indigo as the skin on his cheek began to reknit back into untattooed skin. 'It's not enough indigo to heal all the way through. You'll have to clean up what's left.'

She stared in horror at the piece of inked flesh and skin lying in a puddle of blood on the floor.

'Stay away from those Dayo,' her father said as she cleaned up his face. 'They're trouble.'

'I spend most of my time up the mountains and Galenya's house. I don't go anywhere else.'

He grabbed Yin's wrist. 'We didn't get all the way here for you to be found by accident. The Reds don't know what you look like. Keep your head down and you'll stay alive. Don't make it difficult for me to keep you alive.'

On hearing her father's rebuke, Yin felt red hot rage bubble up in her heart. All her life, she'd been excluded from conversations and decisions that decided her fate. She'd taken it all quietly, without complaint, without so much as a disappointed sigh. The whole while, she had trusted other people with her life, just waiting to *finally* be given the freedom she had craved and this island should have been it—the first safe haven where she could truly be free.

Only now, it wasn't safe for her. She had deluded herself into thinking it could be safe. Nowhere was safe. Not for Dayo. Not for her.

And the worst part? *She didn't even know why.*

She stared at her father disbelievingly, body trembling with anger. 'Maybe you shouldn't have to keep me alive.'

He shot her a glare that should have sent her cowering into the corner of their little house, but today, she found out she didn't care. Her fear was nowhere to be found. In its place, she found a new courage, a profound desire to be in control of her own life, a hunger for freedom.

Her father must have felt this. All the fight left his body and he sighed, exhausted, slouching in a way that was rare. The soldier in him would never have allowed it but here he was, looking small and defeated.

'You think this is the life I wanted for myself?' He said this without blame or remorse. He said this as if it was a simple, inevitable fact, but it hurt her all the same.

She froze, unsure of how to act in the face of this rare show of vulnerability. 'I didn't choose this life either, father.'

'Nor did I or your mother. But this is the life we are dealt.'

'Who is after me? What did I do to them? What was my crime?'

He looked at her, eyes bleak.

'Your crime was being born, Yin.'

# Chapter 7

## Dakila

*Present Day*

Maralita was late. Dakila had anticipated that. His aide had always been unreliable with regards to time, but the man was a skillful soldier and a dependable worker. Dakila figured that the man was late trying to accomplish some menial task for him or for some other commanding officer higher up the ranks, or even for his father, the king.

Maralita, the seventh and youngest son of House Layon across the Kayumalon sea, was an ardent follower of the crown—if not fanatical. Dakila had once suspected that Maralita was one of his father's little birds spying on his queer son, but he kept the man around anyway. He was pleasant to look at in the crimson and black uniform—very, *very* pleasant.

This was one of the few times that it was a good thing that Maralita was late. Dakila didn't want Maralita to see the reaction on his face when he set foot in Dangal's empty room on the second day of the Reaping Festival. His reaction would have given away all his secrets to Maralita, who was far too perceptive for his own good.

The room was in a disreputable part of Castel city, in a district called Tatsulok, but was no doubt the best that this district could offer a prince. Its large open windows with white capiz panes and patterned curtains, gilded foundations, and whitewashed walls, now splattered with blood, were its austere offerings. Dakila caught sight of the bed at the far end and was relieved to see that it was stuffed with feathers instead of straw. However, the smell of the putrid harbour and the unwashed streets below wafted into the room, mixing with the scent of stale wine, dried blood, and urine. It reminded him of an old Kayuman phrase, *'Lalabas at lalabas din ang baho mo'*, translated in the common tongue as 'the stink is bound to come out one day.'

Castel was never the kind of place to wait for 'one day,' city of progress that it was.

Dakila couldn't pinpoint exactly when his brother descended into this. Dangal had always been a happy child, a contrast to Dakila's melancholy childhood. His older brother was the golden boy, the child whose mere presence made everyone smile, the prince whom the common people—from the Dayo servant to the Kayuman noble—loved and adored, the son whom their father doted on and bragged about.

Seedsickness was said to drive one insane before the actual sickness preyed on the body. Their mother was seen talking to thin air towards the end of her short, tragic life, and once every so often, she would scream about the voices in the dark that wouldn't stop talking and begged anyone close by to make them stop. Imperial healers and germachemists couldn't find a cure—though there were rumours that one germachemist had come close in Kolehiyo—and so they resorted to dulling her mind with potions that made her no better than a vegetable on most days, her best days. Their mother died screaming about a burning from within, like she was being consumed from the inside, erased; like an aftermath that was more nothing and less ash.

His brother's descent was quieter, less obtrusive, like the creeping of roots reaching downwards, desperate for water while the leaves reached for light.

Dangal was the happy young boy. And then he was not.

Dakila stood at the doorway of the room, feeling a familiar pang in his chest. Even in the mess, everything in the room looked as if it belonged here, as if this was how it was supposed to be—from the piles of books in the corner, the discarded clothes at the foot of the bed, to the many empty bottles of wine and seedshooters scattered about on the floor. The creation of such messes wasn't unusual for royalty, who were accustomed to having someone else pick up after them. But Dangal had always been different.

It unsettled Dakila. He fidgeted, smoothing down his long, jet-black hair—oiled delicately so that no stray was out of place—straightening out wrinkles on his crimson double-breasted, sleeveless coat that showed off the black tiger claw tattoos up and down his arms, the patterned belt tied around his waist where a ginunting sword and daga dagger hung, and the black boots that he meticulously polished every night.

'Lieutenant Layon reporting for duty, Sir,' Maralita said from behind him in that cheery, sing-songy way of his. 'Sergeants Wagas and Talas are interrogating the staff downstairs.'

Dakila walked into the room, stepping over bloody footprints—one barefoot, the other in boots—and sidestepping books and empty bottles.

'You're late,' Dakila said without looking at his lieutenant as they both made their way to the bed. It was a habit, calling him out for being late. Maralita took it as a greeting.

Maralita stood on the other side of the bed across from him, the Morningstar streaming through the wide-open window and the billowing curtains created a halo of light around the other man who was looking down at the bloody bed.

'No body, Sir?' Maralita asked in a genial tone, as if he was talking to a drinking buddy at a tavern and not his commanding officer. He had an easy way about him, a hidden affable nature that survived the rigorous and vicious training that came with enlisting in Dakila's regiment.

The Kalasag Corps was a special division of the Kayumalon military which reported directly to the king. They were assigned tasks that required specialized skills, resources, and knowledge to accomplish. His people consisted of battle mages, weapon and bomb technicians, assassins, archers, spies, tacticians, and strategists. The Kalasag Corps were deployed on a variety of missions—such as covering up scandals, implanting spies into a rival's court, infiltrating enemy camps, thwarting potential threats, and finding the prince when he snuck out of the palace.

Maralita was among the best minds ever recruited into the Kalasag. He could have easily excelled in administrative positions that didn't frequently endanger him, but he chose the Kalasag because it worked directly with the royal family.

It was this reasoning that made Dakila wonder about how brilliant the man actually was. He didn't look the part of the Kalasag in his crumpled uniform, shorn black hair, cloth-covered arms, and genial demeanor. He was always smiling, always missing the obvious—which worked in Dakila's favor on most days.

'Do you see a body, Lieutenant?' Dakila asked, as he pulled the stained sheets away.

'Never hurts to ask, Commander,' Maralita said, glossing over Dakila's sharp tone and turning his attention to the other parts of the room. He walked around the room, taking mental notes of any specific detail that he thought useful to the scene he was building in his head. Dakila gave his man time to gather his thoughts while he crouched and sifted through his brother's belongings in the trunk next to the bed.

His brother hadn't brought much for his journey from Maylakanon a month ago. He hadn't even brought any of his ceremonial robes and patterns. *Must have figured that he won't need them where he was going,* Dakila thought grimly. He had, however, brought a bag full of seedcoins and paper seedmoney, which he'd buried carelessly under plain clothes in the trunk. It looked as though he had planned to waste away in Castel and never go back home. Maralita stood over the trunk, eyes cataloguing its contents. 'He left everything here. Interesting . . .' he said, trailing off like he had more to say but had decided to hold back.

Dakila stood to face the younger man and folded his tattooed arms across his chest. He hated it when the man held back. 'Theories, officer?'

Maralita swept one last look around the room, checking for any missed details that may prove his theories wrong. Satisfied that there were none, he drew in a breath and presented his case, 'Your brothe— The honorable prince may still be alive, Sir.' He always did like to start with his most optimistic guess. 'However, the blood on the bed, if it's his, shows that he may not have gotten very far. I'll have Wagas and Talas check the streets within the vicinity, but I doubt that they'll find the prince's body.'

'Why do you think so? Maybe he's still out there. Maybe he was abducted by his political enemies—or worse, the mage that destroyed House Talim and Payapa.'

'You surprise me, Commander. Even I lack the imagination to get to that conclusion.'

'It's not impossible, Lieutenant. Only improbable. The assassin has so far killed key members of the Congress, including House Talim. My brother is arguably one of the most powerful men in Congress. Since the work he's done does divest power from the crown, it's not farfetched to assume that someone would want him dead.'

Maralita grinned. 'If I didn't know any better, I'd think you're accusing the king of murder—or trying to throw me off the trail . . . Sir.'

Dakila glared at him, and the man only shrugged.

'No. The murder of House Payapa was a vendetta carried out by an expert and cruel hand.' Maralita shook his head thoughtfully. 'Whoever it was that did this—' Maralita pointed at the blood on the bed. 'It wasn't personal nor political. It was . . . premeditated. It was someone the prince knew, someone he was comfortable with, enough to let them into his room. The discarded women's clothes tell us that there were more than two people here that night. It makes me think that this was set up by the prince himself. He wanted us to find the room in this state, he wanted the possibility of his death to be found here.'

'Nonsense. Everybody knows my brother is a patron of the brothels on this street,' Dakila said indifferently, but he could tell that his statement bothered the younger man. After all, etiquette dictated that the vices of those noble and royal were better left unspoken. Dakila, however, did not care for such pointless decorum. 'Continue, Maralita,' he said, more kindly this time, knowing that the man was partial to the royal family and would have trouble reconciling such truths with his idolized image of them.

'Yes, Sir. There were several women that night, but it seems they were all forced out of the room when someone he knew joined the party. Many of them had to leave behind pieces of clothing. The wine bottles—blue, green, and yellow—suggest that the prince was inebriated that night and thus very vulnerable. The empty seedshooters threw me off for a bit, but my guess is that those shooters were red or indigo. He may have been in a lot of pain before he fled, but you must admit the combination of both colours is unusual. The indigo could have been used to dull the pain, but what did he need the red for? Therefore, I think, maybe it wasn't used by the prince himself but by his guest.' He walked to the bloody footprints on the floor and pointed at it. 'Something bad happened to the prince while he was with his guest, who had to take him out of the room, hopefully to find help.' He eyed Dakila sheepishly, a question in his bright, young face, a reluctance dulling the spark in his eyes. Dakila held the younger man's eyes and nodded, answering his unspoken question.

'My brother may have had the beginnings of seedsickness, Lieutenant Layon,' Dangal said, forcing some gravitas in his voice. 'He has been put on a cocktail of seedshooters, blood transfusions, and heavy medication to slow down the disease, but so far, no germachemist or healer has found a cure.'

'I heard your cousin was close to a breakthrough.'

'But he was expelled from Kolehiyo recently,' he answered, catching himself slipping off the shroud of the General mid-sentence before putting it back on. He cleared his throat, established the valley between commanding officer and subordinate, and said, 'Anything else, Lieutenant?'

Maralita hesitated like he had more questions to ask, but didn't, unsure if he was crossing the arbitrary boundary that Dakila set between work and his personal affairs. The lieutenant was a dog with a bone when given a job. Dakila had come to expect this reaction from his men, Maralita especially, given that his personal affairs did bleed into his work.

'Nothing else for now, Sir. I'll report to you later if Wagas, Talas, and I find anything new,' Maralita said, standing at attention, choosing loyalty to the crown over his duty.

Dakila, satisfied with his lieutenant's decision, left to tell his father what had become of his other son.

# Chapter 8

## Kalem

There was a lot to unpack from Kalem's last month in Kolehiyo.

His small room felt like a dungeon cell deep in Kolehiyo's stone fortress. It had one small window that gave him a full view of the ankles of people walking by in the courtyard. It wasn't much in the way of lighting, but it was enough for ventilation in this room that had become Kalem's germachemical laboratory for his very dangerous experiments with seeds. There was a cot with a trunk for his clothes and personal effects to one side, a desk to the other, bookshelves spanning an entire wall, and piles of books, maps, diagrams, and skin histories he had *borrowed* from the Archive. It should have felt cramped and limiting, but the decade he had spent in this room—ever since he left home for school—had been anything but that.

There wasn't much to pack of Kalem's worldly belongings. Only paltry clothes and school patterns. It was books that really took up space in his trunk, and the menial task of sorting through his things allowed him to get lost in thought and analyse the whirlwind of a week that he had had following his break-in to the headmaster's office.

The masters of the Kolehiyo had deliberated on Kalem's punishment. Many things about his life were in his favor: the fact that he was the king's nephew and a powerful Datu's lone son and heir, the fact that he was from a bloodline that dated back all the way to the first Maragtas kings, the fact that he was favoured by a tenured Master, the fact that, despite his many misdemeanors, he was still the most talented germachemist of his generation.

But these were also the very reasons that convinced him to extend his studies by four more years after finishing the standard six years in school. He should have been graduating in a month, but he'd always thought that extending his tenure here for another four years was an option he could have availed. He had hoped it was an option. Not only to find a cure for the seedsickness that inflicted his bloodline or to stay away from the true duty that awaited him. He had simply loved this life—this simple, straightforward life of an academic.

He was afraid of the life that awaited him at court; he was afraid it would sweep away any traces of who he was or who he could be. He was afraid he would be nothing but the name of the house he was born in. Even his father had been able to find himself in the guise of the war hero he was now known as—the Obsidian Datu—before he had taken his rightful place at the Congress of Datus. So why not him? Why did he not get a chance to do the same?

But as the masters deliberated his fate—in the midst of being interrogated, tested, defended, and maligned for hours on end—he realized what a mistake it was to prolong his stay here. Not only had he failed in his search for a cure in the many tomes of Alaala Archive, but he'd ended up staying for the very reasons that compelled him to leave. He had worked far too hard to be given concessions because of who he was and not what he had accomplished. His fate and duty were inevitable, but his choice had always been his. And he had made some very stupid choices.

Before the masters could reach a consensus, Kalem had found himself informing them that he was dropping out of school to join his father at court. The masters were taken aback, but only by his outburst, not the decision he'd made. He had taken his life into his own hands. His mentor, Master Makabago, would later tell him that the masters had decided to expel him and force him into court after all.

'Headmaster Kaluma will want you to return the books you borrowed from the Archive.'

Kalem startled back, stumbling over a pile of books, and falling on his behind.

He looked over at the doorway of his room where his mentor stood with placid hands clasped in front of him, his skin permanently stained with years of seedmagic use. Despite the tone, he was smiling amicably at Kalem.

'Master Makabago, I didn't hear you come in!' Kalem said, rubbing his back as he stood and rearranged the piles of books that had toppled over when he fell.

'I've been here a good long while, boy,' Makabago said, entering the room, his robe sweeping behind him, and sat at Kalem's desk that was stacked with piles of books for sorting and packing instead of the usual tools, trinkets, seed and dust, formulas, and equipment he'd kept there for daily use.

Those were the first to go in his trunk because they were the easiest to pack. Master Makabago ran his eyes over the desk and commented, 'You've been neglecting your training.'

'Just distracted, Master. Who would have thought that ten years in school would accumulate so much junk?' Kalem said, trying and failing to remember the order in which he wanted to organize the books in his luggage, which was filled to the hilt with more books than he'd known he owned. He decided to start over and unpacked everything already inside the trunk, including his paltry clothes.

'I imagine it would help if you left behind the "junk" that belongs to the school,' Makabago said, watching Kalem.

'Yeah, well . . . What else is the headmaster going to do to me? I'm not his student anymore.'

'Nothing, I suppose. I doubt you're the first dropout to steal from the school.' He then shuffled through the book pile that Kalem had stacked on his desk. 'But I do doubt that you would have time to study godvessel mythology when you go back home.'

Kalem sighed as he stared at his books with a faraway look. 'It just . . . feels wrong to give up on this entirely, Master.' He picked up a book and ran a hand over the embossed title on the hardbound cover. 'This has been my entire life for so long that I don't know who I'd be without it.' He looked to his mentor, waiting for a response, a habit he'd formed in all the years of training with the old man. But Makabago just sat there, staring back at his pupil blankly.

'It's funny to think that it started with a morbid curiosity about my ancestors' past.' He handed the old man the book he was holding. It was a book of fairy tales, watered-down picture-book versions of the books he had found in the headmaster's personal collection. 'It was vanity that brought me here and it's vanity that kicked me out.' Kalem shook his head. 'How arrogant could I be to think that I could solve a problem that my betters couldn't for years? I should have focused on the experimental side of germachemy, not the theoretical.'

'Come now, boy. No need to be overdramatic. Those old geezers had decades of study, and there have been no significant advances in the field since before you were born. You've introduced a branch of study that's better than anything any other germachemist has done in years, even Kaluma.'

'An unproven branch of study that's probably unprovable in my lifetime. Myths are myths for a reason, Master.'

'Some of those myths founded religions, Kalem,' Makabago said.

'Which is why the temples murder people on a regular basis.'

'Most Alagadans would say they are offerings to the gods.'

'To what end? The Alagadan rituals gain nothing from redoing rituals that our ancestors did to create magic out of mortals.'

'Isn't that the thesis of your study? That germachemy is not the origin of the Alagadan discipline, but a branch from a shared power source.'

'An *iteration* of germachemy,' Kalem corrected, feeling like an idiot for correcting his mentor for something theoretical. He'd been particular about the terminologies he used when presenting his studies to the school. What he postulated was a different execution of seedmagic, a more elegant, more powerful iteration gleaned from religion, mythos, and history.

Even common seedmagic was too much for a mortal body and it always spilled out when it was not consumed quickly enough. Seedmagic didn't technically run out, but the body containing it simply proved too small for its infinities. So much had been lost to time in the thousand-year history of Kayumalon, and Kalem believed that there was more out there. 'I think it's time I accept that I've failed, Master.'

His master looked at him like he didn't believe him, and in the back of Kalem's mind, he found himself agreeing. He didn't believe he could truly let go of germachemy for a tedious life in the government. Not when he thought his studies would lead him to the magic that would extend his father's life.

Master Makabago stood from the chair and dusted off his hands, signifying the end of their conversation. His work here was done. 'Well, at least one person will be glad that you're going home.'

Kalem didn't answer, but Makabago knew that he understood. Kalem's father had been pleading with his son to come home and begin learning the ropes of a Datuship. In the end, Kalem shouldn't be so glum. Most failed scholars had nothing to fall back on when they gave up their studies. He was still a Datu's son. He was born to a duty that wasn't his choosing, which really, wasn't that the case for most duties? It was never chosen. It fell upon a person. What a person did with it was what mattered. And Kalem had delayed fulfilling it long enough.

'Sorry, Master. I just rambled about myself there,' Kalem said, not wanting to discuss how he'd also failed his father along with his mentor. 'What did you come here for?'

'I was hoping you'd change your mind.' Makabago walked to the door. 'It's such a shame to lose a talented seedmage to bureaucracy and politics when there's talk of war.'

'The country doesn't need quill quacks like me. It needs heroes.'

'You'd be surprised by how heroic a scholar can be in times of crisis.'

# Chapter 9

## Dakila

*Present Day*

Dakila's name meant 'great,' 'majestic,' and 'glorious' in the old tongue. Dangal, 'honor' and 'dignity.' Sometimes, he told himself that his father had given him the more ostentatious name because it was him whom his father wanted to be great, not his older brother. But that was a lie. Surely the name was meant to be ironic.

'Dakila the Great,' he'd call himself in the mirror, just to get a taste of it, of what he could become.

In that way, he was much like his father.

The day after they found Dangal's room, Dakila found himself in Maragtas Park close to the arena, staring up at the giant copper statue of his father with his kris sword, its wavy blade raised up in one hand in the gesture of a general who had won a battle, and a shield bearing the house sigil of the roaring tiger in the other. The park south of the king's embassy in Castel was crowded with people waiting for dance and musical performances and puppet and pantomime shows. Vendors and hawkers carrying all manner of wares in giant woven bags on their backs, or pulling grey and black carabaos piled high with baskets, mirrors, walis, and knick-knacks set up shop along the wall or under giant betel, coconut, and palm trees. Food carts selling fish balls, barbecued meat, blood, chicken heads, feet and innards, freshly opened coconuts, and *lugaw*[3] were parked near the upscale restaurants where their masters dined. These wafted with the greasy, mouthwatering smell of peasant food, which reminded him of his time as a young sergeant in the Obsidian Sea, in the aftermath of the war, chasing away the Yumbani stragglers from Kayumalon waters. Kayuman, Asuwan, and Dalaket servants, Dayo labourers, and Tikbalang kutseros crowded these stalls.

In a way, his father's statue looked like it belonged in the messy hubbub of the masses waiting for cheap food and even cheaper entertainment. The copper statue itself was hollow inside. This king had never gone to war.

King Duma, third of his name, was the fourteenth king of the Kayumalon Kingdoms, king of the Kayuman, the Tikbalang, and the Dalaket, Oceanmaster of the Asinari merfolk, Tamer of the undead Asuwan, and the longest-ruling monarch of the empire—indisputable now after the discovery of Kalem I's lost journal in Masalanta Island by his great grand aunt, Princess Diwa Maylakan. The first kings of Kayumalon had been three brothers, Maragtas, Kalem, and Batas, three reigns and conquests tucked into one.

Smaller statues of kings past lined the stone pathways that cut through the grass. Even with his father's statue towering

[3] Refers to white rice porridge

over everything in the park, some kings were treated with more reverence; like Maragtas the Conqueror, Maragtas the Peaceful, Sumakwel the Victorious, Duma I the Fortunate, Dumalugdong the Wise, and even Makatunaw the Pretender.

He flattened the wrinkles out of his crimson uniform and then placed a hand on the hilt of his sword, before walking past the statue and straight to the Katapangan Arena, the massive hippodrome at the edge of the park.

His father always went to the arena from the capital when his presence was required in the Congress of Datus in Castel. A spacious balcony with the best view of the fighting arena was reserved for him, and it was where he took meetings with those he deemed worthy of his attention—regardless of their status as rivals or allies. It was considered a great honor to be invited by the king to join him there. Dakila didn't feel honoured to be treated this way by his own father.

He walked to a side entrance into the arena. Katapangan was a structure of big black blocks of stone piled neatly on top of each other to make tiers and stands where the common masses would sit. At the far end was a more elaborate pyramid that opened at a plateau at the top and was shielded from the hot morningstarlight with patterned canopies. The patterns always bore the colour of the highest ranking noble on the island. On regular days, it was usually bureaucrats, ambassadors, or commanders. Today, however, it bore the colours of his father's House—red and gold. Dakila and Dangal had agreed to combine the colours of their parents' respective Houses—red, gold, indigo and silver—for their own patterns.

He climbed the stairs along the side of the plateaued structure all the way to the top where his father sat, stiffly watching the Sinawali Duels below. A man in a uniform like Dakila's, with the exception of longer sleeves, was sitting next to his father in a chair that was pointedly built lower than the throne, and whispering into the older man's ear. Based on the smell alone—herbal, ginger, tangy, and nectarine—Dakila knew that the man was the imperial germachemist and his former combat magic trainer in Kolehiyo, Master Tapang Makabago.

Dakila stood and waited for his turn at the side of the pavilion. A Kayuman came forward and offered Dakila a goblet of blue wine, which he declined. Pale-skinned Dayo servants in grey clothes lined the walls, standing with their heads bowed down, waiting for orders from their masters.

Dakila watched the fighting below; the rush of excitement he felt witnessing the impressive show of combat reminded him of the Reaping ceremony from two days ago. The fighting below had been between a group of Kayuman men, stripped to their loin cloths and tattooed skins, pitted against a horde of Busaws, probably culled from the northern mountains. Short, stout, and burly, the hairy creatures had one black horn in the middle of their foreheads and freakishly long arms and large hands. Most of the creatures had turned increasingly feral as their numbers fell, decimated by the swords of hunters, their orange blood staining the stone floors of the arena. This was merely the cold open to the actual duels between much, much more skilled warriors from all over the country. Dakila recognized one of the younger warriors as he killed the last of the Busaw with a clean slash of his sword. He bit the side of his lip to stop himself from smiling. Maralita proceeded to bow before the king, the head of the Busaw he'd slaughtered raised as an offering.

His father stood up, forcing Master Makabago to stand and draw back to the side while the king acknowledged the victor with a gracious nod before sitting back down. Makabago returned to the king's side, his words loud enough for Dakila to hear. 'Your grace, we can't ignore the Spider Empress now. This is not the time to play games.'

His father cast a sideways glance at Dakila and then said, 'It is not, but we have to play it anyway. We shall speak again before the Congress.' He dismissed Makabago, who bowed and left, nodding to Dakila as he passed him on the way to the stairs.

Pale-skinned Dayo servants cleaned up the bodies scattered on the arena below in preparation for the main duels. Maralita was walking toward the barracks that were under the tiers of seats, laughing with his friends, all of whom were also covered in orange blood. The king summoned Dakila forward with a casual wave of his hand and he strolled over, taking a knee in front of his father, his head bowed, a tattooed arm on his chest.

'Have the courtesy not to show your true skin in my presence,' his father said before Dakila could say anything else. 'You're an officer in my army for gods' sakes.'

Dakila kept his eyes down, but his throat suddenly felt tighter than ever, as if it was trying to stay his sharp tongue. Wounded words that tried to escape were effectively choked down. He could bare his body to this man, and the king would still find it hard to trust him. A long pause fell between them, interrupted by the sounds of the arena, as it exploded with cheers to welcome the duelists.

'Where's my son?' His father finally said without looking at Dakila.

Even now, it hurt Dakila to hear his father speak like that, like he only ever had one son. Dakila looked up from where he knelt, tempted to spite his father for ignoring him, but the rational part of him, the one that told him to fix his rumpled clothes and wipe the sweat off his brow, held him steady. He was not going to give in to his childish impulses. Not this time. Pain must serve a purpose other than spite.

'We found his lodgings in Tatsulok, but he was gone. He left everything he owned.'

'So, you haven't found Dangal?' His father snarled, aiming a vicious glare at his second son.

Dakila matched his father's glare with his own. He always felt like a lesser man in the eyes of his father, never enough, never the one wanted. He shunned all luxuries and privileges afforded to second princes, and instead chose to enlist in the Kalasag Army, foolishly hoping to earn his father's approval. By sheer force of will, he rose up the ranks to be where he was, to be who he was. Now, he knelt before his father, no longer a cowering boy begging his father for help as his mother's agonized screams filled the night sky. His father hadn't deemed his mother, the queen, worthy of a visit even on the night she died. *Not a father, a king. This is who I'm dealing with.* He bowed his head, accepting defeat, even as it tasted bitter. 'No, father. We haven't.'

His father's chin tilted up as he spoke, as if he wasn't looking down enough at Dakila. 'Do you know what it would cost our House should you fail?'

The clash of swords and the grunts of fighting echoed behind him. *Our House. My son.* The contradictions always threw Dakila off. Of course, he knew the cost of not finding Dangal. He, the weaker son, the queer son, the adopted son, the queen's alleged bastard, would then be promised a throne that would be the target of all their House's rivals. Nevertheless, the idea of him on the throne made him feel brave enough to face his father.

'My cousin, that bastard Patas Laya, is moving against me, conferring with my detractors in secret like I don't see what they're doing.' His father's lips tightened to a thin line, eyes narrowing. He took his time talking seemingly enjoying the sight of his son kneeling so low before him. 'I wasn't supposed to become king. No, the gods deemed my older brother Kalem to be the king.' He stood and stepped off the pedestal, taking one slow step after the other so that he stood before Dakila. 'Do you know how I defied the gods?'

Dakila didn't answer, didn't move from his position of weakness before his father. *Not now. Not now*, he told himself in his head. *Pain must serve a purpose.*

'War. My brother died a martyr in the Obsidian War. The idiot led the charge, and the people put me on the throne.'

Dakila frowned. His father didn't fight in that. The Kalasag Crimson Guard of that time hid him in Maylakanon in case his older brother died—and he did. He looked at his father from head to toe. Sickly, thin, and weak, his father was not a man of war, not like Dakila, not like Patas Laya, not like the warmongering king that preceded Duma, Kalem Maylakan. He had his mind, and he had his games. He liked to keep up appearances, hired bards and storytellers to make up stories about his greatness because he had none of it in truth.

'You want the Winter War to happen, like you did the Obsidian War,' Dakila said so low that it came out a hiss.

He stood slowly, seeing a glimmer of the kind of man his father was. 'Now you want Dangal to lead the charge against the Tuki. You're sending him to his death.'

His father seemed smaller now, shriveled. Dakila stood a few inches taller than the man. He must look intimidating in his uniform, his rightly-earned tattoos, his weapons hanging from the leather belt around his waist. His father was weak. He was the lesser man.

'War is imminent. Where a dead king sits on a throne, vultures will not be far.'

'I can be your heir.' Why was he still hungry for this man's approval?

The king scoffed and went back up to his throne, eager to lord over him from a higher place. 'You are no son of mine. And no son of mine is queer.' He sat on his gilded throne and watched a small Dayo man with red hair stab his blade straight in the heart of a taller Kayuman warrior. 'Find Dangal before the Congress of Datus. Our House cannot appear weak.'

And that was the answer. He was not the king's son even when the king forced the country with this truth. Dakila appeared weak to his father. After everything he had done, he was still weak.

After everything, he was still the boy who watched his mother die.

Dakila gritted his teeth and walked away without bowing or acknowledging his father's orders. The king didn't seem to care so why should Dakila?

After all, he was the reason his brother was gone.

# Chapter 10

## Yin

After that odd, horrifying night when her father sliced off the inked skin on his face, Yin had felt like she was in a perpetual state of danger. Like the phantom enemies were lurking in the darker corners of every single street, shop, room. Suddenly, Masalanta became just like any other place she and her father had lived in in the past. It was just another temporary hiding spot. Her father's promise that they could stay here for as long as they needed to didn't seem like a viable option anymore.

She'd come to spend most of her time in the mountains, collecting herbs and fruit for Galenya and staying up there for long stretches of time, just watching the clouds drift over her. Sometimes she even pretended she could read the sky.

She had a favorite spot next to a singular atis tree in a clearing that smelled oddly like mangoes and alatiris. Sometimes, she could hear the mountain talking to her, speaking in tongues she could not understand, but this presence—imagined or not—gave her some comfort that at least she wasn't completely alone. The same thing had happened in the other plantations she'd previously lived on, like the inherent magic of the seedfields gave the places voices to speak with. She spent most of her afternoons here passing the time and pretending the mountain was trying to converse with her.

She'd told Galenya she couldn't help around the house anymore, but she would still be willing to gather fruits and herbs for her. The woman didn't need an explanation, though she did give Yin a wistful, pensive look every night when Yin would knock on her door to deliver her bounty. It made Yin sad that she'd have to leave the only friend she'd made in a long time, and sometimes, in the dark loneliness of empty nights, she even regretted having made this connection in the first place.

Two weeks after the harrowing incident with her father, as she was making her way to her spot, the voices spoke more clearly, like a conduit had been created through which the mountain spoke, not just in tongues but in her tongue, her dialect, her words. There, she found the black dagger stabbed right through the atis' spindly trunk, its branches suddenly lush with sweet, ripe fruit and verdant leaves.

She examined it, circling the tree cautiously to check if the one who had left it there was still in the clearing. From the corner of her eye, she thought she saw shadows lurking in the grove of trees skirting the clearing. However, when she turned to look, there was nothing there but some old, decaying trees. It painted a haunting picture, like the atis tree planted in the very middle of the landscape had stolen all the life from the other trees. Yin, who was constantly warned by her father to be careful, to not tempt fate, to not approach dangerous situations, didn't touch the dagger. But she harvested the fruit, thinking that Galenya might be able to explain this strange phenomenon.

Galenya seemed happy to see Yin again so early in the day. The old woman had somehow gotten Tiyago's younger brother—his name was Feridinan, Yin remembered Galenya telling her a while back—to help around the house and take over as her apprentice. He hadn't completely recovered from his injuries. Still, the boy seemed like he was feeling much better, teasing and bantering with Galenya the way Yin had when she had his job.

Galenya didn't stand from her place in front of the fire, smiling in the direction that Yin was coming from and frowning when something that seemed unpleasant caught her attention.

'You brought me something very dangerous,' Galenya said, sniffing the air and drawing Feridinan's attention from where he was peeling ginger on the floor.

'What is it, *tandang hukluban*?'[4] Feridinan asked, looking over at Yin standing in the doorway with a bag full of atis fruit.

Galenya scowled at the boy and motioned to hit him with a slipper. '*Bastos kang bata ka*![5] Go get us more water!' The boy laughed and ran out of the house, past Yin at the doorway.

'I found atis—' She didn't mention that her secret sanctuary was exactly where she found these fruits. '—while I was collecting herbs. The tree it came from hadn't borne fruit in a while . . .'

---

[4] Means 'old crone' in Filipino

[5] Means 'you stupid rude child/boy' in Filipino

Galenya reached out a hand, gesturing for Yin to give her one, which Yin did. Galenya sniffed at the fruit, squeezed it lightly between her small hands, and pressed it against her ear. Finally, she cracked it open and bit into the white pulpy inside, spitting out the black seeds in the process. She frowned and then looked up at Yin with clouded eyes.

'You found this in the mountain?'

'Yeah.' Yin sat next to the old woman and took out a fruit for herself, which Galenya slapped out of her hands. 'Ow! What was that for?'

'Don't eat it. It's infused with dangerous magic.'

'But you ate it!'

'It won't affect me the same way it affects you, stupid child!'

'What do you—' Yin began to say as she reached for a fruit but was interrupted by a person at the door.

'*Nay* Galenya, I've come to pick up Feri—' He stopped when he saw Yin there. 'Yin, you're here. I . . . We . . . Feri . . .'

'Your brother went to get water at the well,' Galenya said, taking Yin's bag of fruit from her. 'No fruit for you! Go get his brother.' She prodded Yin out the door before spilling the contents of her bag into a basket.

Yin walked out, confused, but Tiyago walked in step with her. 'I'll come with you, Yin.'

What followed were a few minutes of tense walking in silence, passing Reds in their bright red uniforms and menacing tattoos and Dayo with their heads bowed down, eyes downcast. Some of them waved at Tiyago—she recognized them from the beach party. Rejeena specifically, who looked at her from head to toe and then rolled her eyes. Tiyago didn't even seem to notice her.

'I haven't seen you around lately,' Tiyago said, averting his eyes from her and awkwardly running a hand through his red hair.

'I've been spending more time up the mountain,' she answered, smiling, feeling hot blood rushing up her face. He smelled nice, like that first night she'd met him by the beach, like sweet yellow seeds and ocean water, and her mouth went dry at the thought of him standing so close to her again, their bare arms grazing every few steps.

'Right, you gather herbs for the healer,' Tiyago said, then cleared his throat like it would help him feel less awkward. 'I . . . uhm . . . We've got another harvest festival coming soon. All the Kayuman masters will come out to meet the traders at the bay. We get to relax at night.'

She stopped walking and looked at Tiyago. Her previous homes had harvest festivals, too. It was a traders' event meant for merchants to trade goods for seeds with the plantations. At night, the masters threw balls in their grand halls, while the Dayo were allowed to throw end-of-season festivals to celebrate. Dayo were allowed vices, the masters allowed them to host feasts, and party all night till the last moonslight. The next day, the labourers were given the entire day off. It was always a wild night of revelry and debauchery, and the night when many a child were conceived.

'You're new to the island, and this would be your first festival here, and you might not want to go alone so . . .'

She knew exactly where this was going and remembered her father's warning about laying low and keeping her head down. Still, she couldn't deny just how attracted she was to the beautiful boy and had decided that she would spend more time with him, even if it meant disobeying her father.

He hadn't stopped rambling, ceaselessly filling up the tense silence that had ensued. While she took her time to answer, he fidgeted with his hair, drummed his fingers on his shirt, straightened out the wrinkles this made on his shirt and looked at Yin like she was giving him indigestion. 'It's going to be a lot of fun. There will be so much food and drink, you could eat your weight in Lechon if you want. The masters will also bring out the good wine—'

'Are you asking me to go with you to the fiesta?' She asked abruptly, interrupting his ramble.

'I . . . Why . . . Yes, please go with me to the fiesta?' He asked, looking bravely into her eyes like he'd just asked the most important question of his life.

The confirmation made her insides tingle with little pinpricks of electricity surging through her veins. It felt nice to be wanted. It felt really nice to be noticed. It felt really, really nice to be noticed by someone so beautiful as Tiyago, so before her father's voice in her head—or any other voice of reason really—stopped her, she nodded.

# Chapter 11

## Dakila

*Thirteen Years Ago*

Dakila found Dangal alone in his room, holding a bottle of blue wine.

He was not the same when he returned after months of being gone. Barely smiling, barely doing the things he loved, barely leaving his room, even for Kolehiyo. Hair overgrown, beard hiding his face, clothes disheveled. The sour scent of stale alcohol and blue seeddust was pervasive. It was like all the joy had been taken out of him. Dakila barely recognized him.

He left the palace often, even after he'd gone missing for months, returning only when their father's soldiers dragged him back home.

Dakila stood at the door, waiting to be acknowledged. From his seat on the floor by the floor-to-ceiling window that overlooked the palace grounds Dangal cast him an absent look, a weak and sad smile pulling up the corners of his lips. He looked at his younger brother as if he wasn't just a ten-year-old boy, as if he didn't know him.

'Did you know Maragtas the Peaceful was the first Kayumalon king to divest power from the throne? He established the first Congress of Datus because he did not want to turn into his father. You'll learn all about it in Kolehiyo.' Dakila didn't understand. Dangal drank dulling, blue wine. 'He didn't want to turn into his father.' He laughed. 'Maragtas the Peaceful did not want to become Maragtas the Cruel.' He laughed like it was the funniest thing in the world.

'I don't understand, *kuya*,' Dakila said, still not moving from his spot. 'Father said you were only being stubborn . . . that you'd come home eventually. You'll always come crawling back home, he said.'

Dangal frowned. 'Father doesn't know what he's talking about. This place hasn't been home even before our mother died.'

'But what about me, Dangal?'

That gave Dangal pause, the bottle midway to his lips. He put it down and stared at his brother, aghast, pitying, disgusted, and annoyed all at the same time. His mercurial mood vacillated between a fond gentleness and a rigid harshness. Dakila could not predict what would come next. His brother had never looked at him this way before, like he was a wayward fly landing on fresh rice cake. 'You? What about you? If it weren't for you, Caritas—' He stopped, and drew in a breath, and another, and another, the way princes were taught to rein in what they felt when at court. 'I'm sorry, Dakila. It's not your fault. I just have a lot on my mind.'

Dakila stepped further into the room, walking up to his brother, close enough so he could hear him better, but far enough that Dangal wouldn't be able to reach him with his outstretched hands—or fists. He had grown taller over the years, but he still was a small boy compared to Dangal. 'What happened to Caritas?'

Dangal turned away with the murmur of an 'I don't know' passing his lips. 'We were going to run away, but Father found out and sent her away.'

'Where did she go?'

'I don't know.'

Dangal relaxed on the floor, eyeing Dakila standing before him from head to toe. Dakila recoiled under his gaze. He looked up to his older brother for everything. He was the golden boy, the first prince. The man who held the moons in the palm of his hand. He couldn't take seeing him like this, fallen so far from the pedestal that he seemed like a stranger wearing his brother's skin.

*'May tenga ang lupa may pakpak ang balita,'* the servants whispered about him, and it finally clicked what they meant, what he'd done.

'You love her,' Dakila said, head swimming as recalled the events of that day. 'I told Father to stop Caritas from leaving.' He walked toward his brother and knelt in front of him, finally understanding why he looked at him that way. The truth washed over. 'It was my fault,' he said, stammering. 'Did Father . . . did Father kill her?'

Dangal tore his eyes away from Dakila, staring out the window and at the seven moons in the sky. 'Please leave me, Dakila.'

'No, I'll find her. I'll beg Father to send her back. I'll—'

'Just go, Dakila!' Dangal said, louder than he'd intended. He picked up the bottle and drew in a deep breath before drinking. 'I want to be alone.'

And so, with a heavy heart, Dakila left his brother alone.

# Interlude

*After the Payapas' Massacre*

It was too late for this small winter town of Lamigin in Tukikuni country. The Shadow of Death came for it and left behind the blackened bones of homes and the decaying corpses of people in its wake.

The carnage was terrible, but it was the silence permeating the place that punctuated the palpable horror. It was like the inhale of a breath that was never exhaled. Like a sudden rainfall stopped before the first drop hit the ground. Like the closing of a book before the last page was turned. Lives were lived here and then there were none.

JinWun rode up on her white mare through what remained of the small streets of this small town. She stripped off her white fur coat and let it hang from the leather belt around her waist, next to where twin iron swords hung. It left her in her thin cotton robes that were doing their best to protect her from the winter chill.

Her veins were lit a brilliant emerald green, the magic keeping her warm in an otherwise warmer section of her country. Her fire fox god, Yewu, sprung around her head like it was climbing a flight of stairs, its tail leaving a trail of glittering green mist behind him. Her bob-cut hair stuck to her face, wiry and crackling dry against the cold.

Behind her was a singular soldier in the white-and-brown uniform of the Tukikuni military. She had only brought one with her on this reconnaissance mission. There wouldn't be much to report back. There wasn't much left of this town. The question was who did it. Power like this wasn't common seedmagic, and even that was rare in these parts. Kayumalon had an almost absolute monopoly on seedmagic, which has made the archipelago country practically impregnable, untouchable, unconquerable.

This was bad for the barren winter countries like Tukikuni, which had relied on trading, pillaging, and stealing from other weaker neighboring countries to survive and had to fend off other invaders from taking what little they had. Powerful countries like Kayumalon need not worry about outside threats, but Tukikuni, Lasta, or even Yumbani were no threats to them at all. Yumbani, during a period of drought and famine decades ago, tried to steal from Kayumalon by sea and failed spectacularly. It was the threats within that they had to worry about.

Lasta and Tukikuni fought each other for resources, and the Tuki would have been finished had it not been for the Spider Empress, who somehow brought magic to the country—but at great cost to her.

JinWun stopped in the open, now levelled, space, which was covered in a layer of snow so deep that it reached up to her horse's ankles. Her companion, with pale, almost bluish skin, almond-shaped eyes and green irises, barely a beard, and thick hair tied in a knot above his head, stopped his own brown horse next to hers and pulled down the thick, fur-lined hood of his coat with gloved hands. He was young, too young for war, but the Tuki didn't live long enough to reach an age that would be considered old. Only the seedblessed, like JinWun, ever lived as long as she had.

'Gon, check for survivors,' JinWun said as she surveyed the surrounding ruins of buildings in what she remembered to be the town's main square. Some of the structures maintained the integrity of their lower floors, and though she had hoped that there would be survivors who had witnessed the events that led to the fall of this town, she could feel in the still air there would be none.

'Yes, Captain,' Gon said, riding up ahead to check the ruins, splashing up snow around him as his horse tried to gallop through it.

***'It's not one of ours,'*** Yewu said, settling on Jin's shoulder.

*'No, it's not,'* Jin said, closing her eyes, focusing all sensory feeling on searching for odd vibrations in the air, anomalies that only seedgod magic can create. *'None of my siblings have this power.'* In her mind's eye, she saw herself floating in the void where she first met Yewu when she fused her soul with his.

***'It's an ancient power.'***

*'An ancient death god perhaps.'*

***'It hasn't been awake for as long as we have.'***

*'A dangerous god then. Only the Kayuman would have such a dangerous god. It was awakened recently.'*

***'Recent is an understatement to mortals. Perhaps the Lastans seek revenge.'***

*'It can't be the Lastans. This town is too small, too far, and too insignificant to make a statement.'*

**'So, the Kayuman then. Why?'**

*'I don't know. We have nothing that they could want.'*

**'We have godvessels. We have the Spider Empress.'**

*'And so do Lasta and Yumbani.'* Minor gods, but gods nonetheless. Jin opened her eyes again, her senses pointing her to the left side, an eerie thrumming of magic that echoed her own calling to her. Godvessel magic was showy by nature—not unlike common seedmagic that required chemical help. Not only did seedgod magic make its presence known in a mage's body by way of lighting up the veins, it also called out to other instances of magic around them. It was why the Spider was such a fearsome monarch, queen of a barren land though she may be.

No one knew exactly where these gods came from, but their existence could be traced back to the early Tuki nomad tribes that roamed the country before the coming of the Spider Empress. All the Tuki knew was the gods needed mortal vessels to exist in this realm. They fused their spirit with mortal souls. In exchange, these gods granted their godvessels access to their magic.

The Spider was fused with more than one god—six in fact. And she had six more godvessels under her command, including Jin, just waiting to be fused with the Spider. *'The Kayuman wouldn't try to challenge the Spider. It would start a world war.'*

**'Which makes this attack odd.'** Fire fox paused. A silence that was loaded with dark implications about the most powerful country in the world.

*'Unless they want to start a war.'* Panic rose in Jin's chest as the pieces matched up in her head. She commanded her horse to

run toward the direction of the dark anomaly, the herald of war, the herald of death. She could still be wrong. This could just be another freak accident of magic, as was the case for any other seedgod awakening. But despite her reassurances to herself, *she knew.* Every fibre of her being, every instinct she'd earned in her long life was telling her that the situation was exactly what it looked like. And the horror wreaked on this town was only a prelude to the horror that was to come.

The Shadow stood among the ruins of a fallen church. It was a church to a wind god, the east wind, to which the people prayed for warmth, hot enough to make the soil arable. He was holding the black ceremonial dagger towards the light streaming from the run-down ceiling, watching the blade absorb the daystarlight even as the weapon cast a shadow over his pale face, cracked by black veins.

'It's strange to find a godvessel's blade in a temple on full display,' the Shadow said, his dark cloak splayed out on the white snow as more white dust trickled down from the sky. 'In my country, priests use replicas of blades in their rituals.'

'My people don't sacrifice lives for religion,' Jin answered flatly as she got down from her horse to approach the man. 'Kayuman do. Your people.'

He lowered the blade and turned to fully face her. He was at least two heads taller than her, with broad shoulders and a large chest that dwarfed her in comparison. He wore black all over, and not even an inch of his pale skin was visible under the layers of dark clothes. 'No,' he said, pulling up a sleeve with a gloved hand to emphasize his pale skin. 'But I suppose you can call anyone born in Kayumalon as Kayuman. I'm not though.'

'What have you done?' Jin asked, approaching the man slowly.

He averted his gaze from her as if he was genuinely ashamed of what he had done. 'I tried to keep some of them alive as witnesses, messengers to your queen, but I figured it would send a clearer message if I stayed to tell you what happened here.'

'You did this of your own volition then?'

He nodded. 'One of the few horrific things I've done without magical coercion.' He sheathed the dagger and clipped it to his belt. He looked up at the collapsed roof, at the demolished foundations, at the destroyed pieces of furniture, all of it still trailing smoke and grey dust of disintegrating decay, and he smiled, looking ashamed of his handiwork. 'But it does look like I was commanded to do so by my master, doesn't it?'

'Why? Why this town?'

'It was a small town. Far from the crowded capital. Insignificant. Forgettable—unless a witness came forward of course.'

'But the atrocities you've committed here are not insignificant. It's an act of a powerful country inciting war with a smaller country.'

'I guess only you will know if a war is coming.'

'And you think I'll let you play me?'

He grinned, stealing a sideways glance at her as he watched snow begin to fall again. 'I don't. But think of it as serendipity.'

'I don't understand.'

'You of all mages would know what it's like to be at the mercy of an unscrupulous master. Our powers used against our will. Our wills bent and deformed to fit someone else's. Our lives not our own. Slaves of a broken system.' He levelled a look at her that felt like it was taking daggers to her soul. 'I want to break that system. I'm done being a pawn in someone else's game. I am a vessel of a dangerous god. We *are* gods. You have a choice here, Fire God. Tell your master about what really happened here and save your country from a protracted war . . .'

He paused, looking at her as if gauging her reaction to this, trying to read her face for understanding or agreement. She raised an eyebrow at him, a gesture for him to continue.

He grinned, knowing that he had piqued her interest. 'Or lie. Tell your Spider that the winds of war are coming for Tukikuni. Tell her that the Kayuman king is hungry for power, for domination. Tell her that it is only a matter of time that she too becomes the Kayuman king's slave.'

It dawned on her then why the Shadow didn't need survivors here. 'You waited for me to come to you. You wanted me to come to you. You were sure that I would conspire with you on this.'

'Death is both ending and beginning. I have nothing to lose, and you have everything to gain, Fire God.'

'I know what I can gain from this. What I don't understand is your motivation for this. Why start this war against your own country?'

He paused, the amusement on his face replaced by a fury that was not divine but so very human. 'I want to see my master suffer. I want him to lose everything he has gained by misusing me.'

If she had doubted the Shadow's motivation, she didn't doubt it now. In this she saw his mortality, their shared humanity, the very tethers that kept them human even with the gods flowing through their veins. 'The town you destroyed is too insignificant. The Spider won't believe that the Kayuman could be so careless.'

'It's why I waited for you. I needed assurance that the correct message would be delivered.' He tapped the hilt of the dagger he had stolen. 'Tell the Spider that this was only a taste of what's to come. Tell her that more gods will be awakened for this. Tell her what she needs to start a war.'

JinWun knew. She had known for a long time what could force the Spider to attack. Finally, after much thought, after remembering everything she had to gain and lose from this, she nodded, slowly, as if it would delay their plans longer. 'Are you sure about this?'

He grinned, that trickster god back, the humanity gone. His body morphed into smoke and shadow. A disembodied voice spoke, *'I am an instrument of death. It is only fitting that I meet my demise in war.'* The dark cloud rose up into the sky, trailing a stream of shadow below it. *'We shall meet again.'*

She watched the Shadow of Death fly higher and higher until it was no different from the storm clouds and snow clouds that drifted over the small town, raining down petals of snow over it.

'A godvessel did this, Captain?' Gon said, coming up seemingly from out of nowhere. 'Was it sent here by the Kayuman?' *How much had he heard?*

Here Jin had a chance to change the course of history, to save the world from pain and suffering at the hands of the powerful. But the death god was right. She was pure power herself. Why did mortals get to dictate the fate of the world when she had the power to take back the reins of her life and love?

'Yes. They mean to go to war,' she lied, her words heavy on her tongue, carrying the weight of changing the world forever.

# ACT 2

# Chapter 12

## Yin

Yin knew without a shadow of a doubt that her father would forbid her to go to the fiesta—not since more Reds had come to the island and were patrolling the streets and seedfields—so, she decided, she wasn't going to let him know her plans.

She had expected to leave the island soon, which made sense given the increased guard, but her father had not even suggested it. When she asked, he answered that it would be more suspicious to leave now. She sensed that there was something else he wasn't telling her, and somehow, she knew it was the reason they needed to stay here for an extended period of time. He did say, before they landed here on the Dalaket ship, that they could live here for as long as they needed to, but that only made sense if her father had expected that their life in hiding would end here. And that wasn't happening any time soon.

Yin's father had kept watch of the military activity in the island, making note of all the additional ships that were docked at the port and then formed a barricade of sorts around the island, in formations that made it seem like they were expecting an attack from the outside.

The Reds were agitated, more prone to doling out punishment to the Dayo labourers even without provocation. More and more Dayo came to Galenya's house with wounds and injuries, a constant stream of wounded that depleted Yin's regular haul even before the day was done. She had made quite a few additional trips up the mountain to get Galenya more herbs and supplies. This meant that she was reaching home later than usual and on a few occasions, cutting it dangerously close to curfew. It was also getting harder to find herbs as she'd picked her usual spots clean of their offerings.

Her atis tree, however, had remained lush as ever, and though she was tempted to try some—she imagined sometimes that the tree itself was calling her to try some, she didn't, remembering Galenya's warning.

Through all this, Yin determinedly kept her head down, and as a result, the Reds generally left her alone. Sometimes, on the way to Galenya's house from her mountain hike, she would catch Tiyago in the main plaza, where a giant Kanlungan tree stood, raining yellow petals all over the place. He'd be returning from the fields after a hard day's labor, and when he caught sight of her, his face would break out in the most gorgeous smile, making her heart flutter.

Every time she saw him, her excitement about going to the fiesta with him rose, making her more determined to follow through with her plans despite her father's wishes. She had decided that she would wait for her father to retire after a long day's work, making sure he saw her in her own sleeping mat, before sneaking out. She had anticipated him working late during this time of the year. He would be busy tracking the yields of every harvest and ensuring the right quantity was distributed to the correct traders' ships before the day ended.

Plans in place, tucked snugly into her sleeping mat, she waited . . . and waited . . . and waited . . . until she was sure that the fiesta in the plaza was well underway and Tiyago must have assumed that she had abandoned him and therefore found another girl to go with. The thought had her stomach twisting in knots.

More time passed until all the moons were high in the night sky and her father had still not come home. Worry ate at her. Her father never stayed out this late, and the last time she could remember this happening, years ago, she remembered how he'd sent word to her mother. She looked out the window and saw Reds casually strolling down the street. She ducked out of view when one of them turned her way.

What was happening? Reds didn't usually tighten patrols on fiesta nights in the villages. Security was always concentrated on the docks during these seasons. She had a bad feeling about this night. Even the wind felt wrong.

She took a scarf—picking her mother's patterned woven one for luck or maybe for her protection from the afterlife—hanging from a hook on the back of the door and wrapped it around her head to cover her face before walking out the door. Her first thought was to go to the docks where her father was working that day.

She made a plan in her head, tracing pathways she could take to get there. The garrison was closest to the usual path that labourers took daily. The gates closing off the docks from the town proper would have the most Reds standing guard. The dirt road cutting through the mountain pass was too long and dark, but of the three routes it was the most viable. She was used to the mountain, knew its rocks and crevices and bends and curls. She had the best chance down that path. The more she thought about it, the more she had to convince herself that this was a good idea, the more she could see that all of them had one common fatal flaw. There were just far too many Reds, and what she had planned to do was the complete opposite of what her father had told her to do: Keep her head down. Stay out of trouble. Don't let the Reds notice her.

*'Psst!'* A voice called from the foliage lining the street, and for a second, she thought it was a nuno—a grotesque, vengeful dwarf that lived in ant hills—or worse a Red, until she saw a flash of red hair over the hedge. Her heart skipped a beat and she ran to Tiyago, crouching behind the bush next to him just as the two Reds who had earlier passed by her house went back down the path.

'Hi,' he said shyly and earnestly. He was dressed in patterned woven pants, probably his best piece of clothing, and he had tied his red hair in a neat low ponytail hanging down to the base of his neck.

She answered him with the same shyness, 'Hi . . . What are you doing here?'

'I came to check on you. Everyone's in the plaza for the fiesta. The masters just brought out the Lechon,' he said.

'I can't leave yet. I'm waiting for my father. He hasn't come home.'

'He's in a meeting with the masters. A very important nobleman came today, one of the king's closest aides. He hasn't come out of the main mansion since.'

'Oh . . .' she said, looking over the plaza tree, lit up from below with all colours of seedlamps brought out for the occasion, and then at the white mansion before turning back to Tiyago. 'He's safe?'

'Of course, he's safe. All they do is talk about money and harvest yields in there.' He looked up over the edge, watching the two Reds go further and further away from them. 'That's why there are more Reds today. After what happened to the Payapas, the noble families aren't taking any chances.'

'So, there's no danger?'

He shook his head then grinned. 'Only if the Reds catch us outside of the plaza.' He offered his hand to her. 'You ready to come to your first Masalanta fiesta?'

She looked over at the mansion again, that knot in her stomach twisting again. 'I think I should wait for my father . . .'

'Your father won't be out of there until morning. Masalanta is the biggest seedplantation in all of Kayumalon. The negotiations usually last till morning.' He took her hand in his. 'Come on? Please? I swear I'll get you back here before he returns.'

She turned her gaze to him this time, searching for the lie or the trickery in his face. How much did she know of this boy to trust him? But then he smiled and stole a peck, and suddenly all doubt went out the window, along with, apparently, her common sense.

'Okay. But just until midnight.'

# Chapter 13

## Dakila

*Present Day*

'We found *a* body.'

Dakila turned to the man lying on his side, his elbow propping up his head.

'*A* body?' Dakila said, turning back to the mirror to continue unbuttoning his uniform.

'Yeah. Right on the border of Tatsulok and Ani districts. Not your brother's, thank the gods. An ageing, minor noble from the south.' He said the last part with a yawn. Maralita stretched out on the bed, muscles rippling, coiling and uncoiling, under the incandescent light of the yellow glowlamp, which wafted the nectarine scent of yellow seedmagic—aphrodisiac magic when used right. Dakila watched the younger man in the mirror, stared at the golden glow of his brown skin even under the yellow light, at his dark hair on white pillows, at his face twisted in blissful abandon.

With eyes closed, Maralita grinned. Dakila's jaw dropped, his hand gripping a button tight, realizing what the beautiful man on the bed had done. Dakila shook his head, took off his uniform quickly, and climbed on top of Maralita.

'I see *a* body right here.' He pinned Maralita's hands over his head and lowered his lips to Maralita's, savoring the nectarine taste of Charmer's wine on his tongue. Maralita moved, testing Dakila's grip on him, but Dakila held steadfast, snug against his lover's body. The boy melted into Dakila, pulling him down, tasting his skin, owning his body like a conqueror finding new land to take, two bodies turning into one, lost in passion and pleasure and the intoxicating throes of control.

'You had a bad day. I can tell,' Maralita said after, panting, head on Dakila's heaving chest. 'What happened with your father?'

Dakila didn't answer, idly running his hand through the boy's hair. He looked out the window of his room. Rather than staying at the emperor's embassy—as was his right—whenever he was on the island, he'd instead taken up residence on the top floor of an elaborate building in Bisig, an upscale district near Maragtas Park. His flat was small compared to his rooms in the Maylakan embassy, miniscule compared to his chambers in Maylakanon's capital. But it was quaint and homey, with its wooden furniture, the tapestries on the wall, and the stained capiz shells embellishing the windows. He had a good view of the park and Katapangan Arena, which was lit from the inside by larger glowlamps of the seven seedmagics. Duels usually went well into the night, followed by a feast in the park. Tomorrow, there would be a parade for the victors of the duels on the way to the temples where they would pray to the new god.

'*Irog*, talk to me,' Maralita said, propping himself up on his elbows so that he was looking into Dakila's eyes. It wasn't so much a command as a plea. 'I worry.'

'Don't. It's just more of the same. You know my father.'

'I worry anyway. I know you.' Maralita's eyes held his, and Dakila fought the urge to look away. Maralita had a way of making people show their true selves around him. He knew just the right buttons to press and the right time to press them. It was an instinct that Dakila wished he had himself. It was an instinct Dakila wished wasn't near him when he held so much close to his chest.

He sat up and picked up a bottle of the blue wine from the side table. 'My father wants to find my brother before the Congress.'

Sighing, Maralita sat up as well and leaned back into the headboard. 'That's so soon.'

Dakila drank from the bottle, feeling the cold, soothing magic surge through his veins, making them glow a faint blue.

Maralita took the bottle from him and drank, too. 'Why the rush? Your brother has disappeared for longer periods of time before this.'

'I don't know. My father is planning something, and the Tuki threat coming from the northern borders is the least of his problems.'

Dakila was never one for politics. He preferred the honesty of sword and shield over the double-edged blade of words. He just didn't have the head for it the way that Dangal did, but he understood Kayumalon's system of government well enough to know the many strategies and gambles at play from all sides of this ridiculous theatre of politics.

Though Kayumalon had a monarchical government, it wasn't ruled by an absolute monarchy. Clever statesmen and politicians and relatives from the same Maragtas bloodlines had over time divested that absolute power to a Congress of Datus, composed of the leaders of the ten major regions of Kayumalon—the four Kayuman provinces, Lakanlupa, Lakantabi, Maragtas Isles, and Maylaya, the three Dalaket provinces, Salamin, Mahakit, and Ilogani, and the three remaining strangelords' provinces, Olimawi of the Asuwan, Asinar of the Sirena, and Lupang Bakal of the Tikbalang.

'So? We have the most powerful army in the world. I don't see what the Congress is worried about. Tukikuni barely won against the Lastans. And that's Lasta. What chance do they have against us?'

'I don't think the Congress is just about the war against the Tuki, given that the Obsidian Datu called for it himself. The Imperial Germachamist seems to think that we shouldn't underestimate this Spider Empress.'

Maralita stood and went to pick up Dakila's uniform. 'Of course, it's magic. It's always about magic. Whatever it is that pushed this Empress to go south after the war with Lasta, it must have put her on a deadline. Kayumalon is too powerful a country to be invaded. Not by Yumbani. Not by the Lastans. And especially not by the Tuki. They'd be stupid to do it unless they have to.' He folded the crimson uniform neatly and placed it in the rattan closet. 'Or unless they have a weapon that evens the odds.'

Dakila hesitated, suddenly wary of the direction in which this conversation was going. Instead, he said after a long pause, 'Did you find anything useful today? Anything that could lead us to Dangal?'

'As a matter of fact—' Maralita went to the table, picked up the burlap bag on it, and took out a dry blood-stained sash with a red, gold, indigo, and silver pattern. 'I found this in a pawnshop in Ani district. Sold by a streetwalker according to the store owner.'

Dakila bolted upright, recognizing the pattern, his throat tightening, his heart racing in his chest. 'And where is this streetwalker?'

Maralita put the sash down on the table, folding it so that it hid the stains. 'I sent Wagas and Talas to find her. She should be in the garrison before we get there in the morning.' He turned to Dakila, a worried look on his face. 'Are you all right, Dakila?'

'I'm fine,' Dakila said, slumping back into bed, mind racing. How much could he ask Maralita before giving himself away? Maralita was smart. He was excellent at his job, but the man was a slave to his passions, his emotions. Dakila wasn't sure how he felt around this man. He was free to be himself with him, to let go of the uniform, of the lie he'd had to wear all his life. He often wondered how much of his walls he could let fall for Maralita, how much he'd let him see and at what point the other man would be forced to turn away in disgust. Without the facade, even Dakila didn't like what he saw in himself.

'You're a good liar, Dakila, but I'm not letting this one slide so easily. Tell me.'

Dakila sighed. He couldn't very well tell him everything, but he could open his heart to the man.

'My father said something today.'

'What?'

'It's a thing that he has only implied in the past.'

'What?' Maralita frowned as if he'd found something unusual in Dakila's face. He knelt next to the bed, close to Dakila. 'You know, it's very unlike you to mince words. Even with me. If I didn't know any better, I'd think you were hiding something.'

Dakila turned away and swallowed the lump in his throat. 'You are no son of mine. And no son of mine is queer."

Maralita slumped on his haunches, his shoulders dropping as if pulled down by an invisible weight. 'He knows about us?'

Dakila shook his head. 'It doesn't matter if he knows.'

'Of course it does,' Maralita said quietly turning away and leaning back on the edge of the bed. 'What . . . what did you say?'

'Nothing,' Dakila answered flatly.

'Should we stop—' Maralita asked tentatively, only to be cut short when Dakila didn't let him finish.

'You're way too in love with the monarchy,' he said, partly a joke, partly a statement of truth. Dakila sat next to Maralita on the floor and leaned against his shoulder. 'You know I love you, right, Maralita?'

'I'm loyal to my king and my country. I love *you*.' Maralita took Dakila's hand in his, intertwining their fingers and kissing the back of it. 'We'll find your brother. Or we'll find his body.'

Dakila drew in a breath. He knew better. There wasn't going to be a body.

# Chapter 14

## Kalem

*Less Than a Month Ago*

'I've not much time left, son,' Kalem's father said, smiling, a piece of mango rice cake halfway to his mouth. 'I'm dying.' The white and yellow sticky cake disappeared into his mouth.

His father seemed remarkably smaller compared to the last time Kalem had seen him. The tattoos on his face seemed less menacing, less imposing. Without his headdress, his thinning grey hair fell in loose stringy clumps over his forehead and neck. The sword, named Obsidian Blade after the Obsidian Sea where he won it from the Yumbani, leaned on the wall, its black blade and hilt tucked in a Dalaket living wood scabbard and its indigo, spherical glass pommel reflecting and absorbing the many lights of the coming night. It was an unusual sword with a curved black blade, embossed with symbols in another language, and an ornate black hilt—certainly nothing like any sword made by a proper Kayuman metalsmith. This was the hero of the Obsidian War, and he was smiling jovially at his son like he'd just told a stupid joke.

'You say it like you're happy about it, father,' Kalem said, nursing a cup of salabat tea and ignoring the platter of sweet breads and rice cake laid out before them, and sitting across from his father at the table. They were in a dessert shop called The Himagas in the upscale Punyagi district near Maragtas Park and the Katapangan Arena. Datu Patas loved this shop so much that the store owner reserved a private seating area on the balcony for him whenever he was in the city. Kalem didn't have the appetite to eat anyway, and he'd been delaying telling his father about his departure from school. His father had always had high expectations of his only son. He had never said it out loud, but Kalem knew he'd broken his father's heart when he accepted the position as Makabago's apprentice instead of going home after his primary education in Kolehiyo was done.

His father waved a dismissive hand and, laughing, said, 'I won't know if I am until it actually happens.'

'Must you joke about it, Father?' Kalem said, watching him pour yellow nectarine wine into a goblet.

'Did Tapang lash your behind so hard he left the stick up there?' His father answered after downing the contents of the cup.

'Master Makabago hasn't given me lashings since my third year, Father. Will you ease up on the wine?'

'Lighten up, son. I'm just happy to see you. Have you been eating right? Drinking enough indigo?' his father said, placing cakes on Kalem's empty plate.

'You know too much wine isn't good for you. Drink salabat instead.' Kalem pushed his mug toward his father across the table. 'Ginger tea will be better for your health. No withdrawals. No addiction.'

His father picked up the mug, sniffed at it, and cringed at the gingery scent of salabat. He pushed it unceremoniously back to Kalem with a hearty laugh and popped a small square of sapin-sapin, a kind of colourful, sticky rice cake, into his mouth. He waved for the room servant to bring in more wine—the healing indigo this time, no doubt a jab at Kalem's 'better for your health' bit.

The Morningstar was already sinking deep in the west. It was too late for merienda and too early for dinner, but his father was eating dessert. His father, the Datu of Maylaya, fearsome warrior of the Obsidian Sea, and cousin of the king, had a raging sweet tooth.

'I met Panday at our Castel embassy. Says you're just as insufferable as you were back home, and you're more a danger to yourself than any monster or man he's protecting you from. What's the point of having a bodyguard if you don't let him go with you to Kolehiyo, son? Do you even leave the school? Or at least check in on our embassy here?'

'The Dalaket twins you hired to manage the embassy do fine without me.' Kalem sighed, fidgeting with the textured clay mug of salabat his father had rejected with both hands. It wasn't hot anymore. He raised his eyes up to his father, who was watching him gently. A pang of guilt shot through his heart. He cleared his throat. 'And I don't need a bodyguard. I'm at school all the time.'

'How will you give me grandchildren then if you stay cooped up in that lab of yours?' His father drummed his fingers on the table like he was counting time.

Kalem felt blood rise up his face. 'Father!'

'I'm just saying. You won't meet nice girls if you don't put yourself out there.' His father laughed.

'I . . . I . . .' Kalem stuttered. He hadn't given it much thought. He knew that people in their position weren't given that much say in who they loved and spent the rest of their lives with. Marriages were no different than contracts—simple transactions between partners with mutual or complementary needs. He'd assumed that he'd likely marry some rich princess of a neighboring Datuship or a powerful bannerman's daughter. 'Seed's honest truth, father, I thought you'd marry me off to whomever you think is most advantageous to our Datuship. So, I never even considered it.'

Kalem squirmed from the way his father was looking at him, like he was reading a particularly difficult book. 'Is that what you want, son?'

'I thought that's what you wanted,' he answered quietly, turning away from his father.

'It doesn't matter what I want, son. I'm dead in a few months, a year tops. I want you to be happy in that regard at least.'

'You really should stop joking about dying, Father. It's never funny.' He cast a serious, warning look at his father.

'Who says I was joking?' His father shrugged and popped another square of rice cake in his mouth. 'Death is inevitable for all of us. For me, it's even more likely. I'm old and sick. I just want to make the most of the time I still have. I want to see my grandchildren before I die or at least meet their mother.' His father sighed, seeing the reluctance still on Kalem's face. 'Is it because you like men?'

Kalem shot his father a look, frowning and confused.

'I'll accept you no matter what, son.'

Kalem thought about it. He's never really given it much thought, if he was being honest with himself. Why bother considering it when he thought his entire life was mapped out for him and he was just doing all he could to delay the inevitable? But then, his father had just basically said that this part of his life at least was in his hands. He felt like another door had been opened to him, one that he didn't think was there all along, and he didn't know how to answer.

His father smiled patiently. 'Tell you what, son. Come with me to the Datu's Ball the night before the vote, and I'll give you a day off before we leave for Maylaya. If you really want an advantageous marriage for your reign, you'll have plenty of chances of meeting the right girl—or boy—there, hopefully one you could be happy with for the rest of your life.'

'Why do you insist on this, Father? You know I don't want to be Datu.'

'Love without duty is an empty promise. Duty without love is vanity,' his father said simply, as if that was answer enough.

'I don't have a choice, do I?' He asked, not really meaning it. Love was the least that his father could give him, especially when he couldn't have everything he wanted.

His father blinked in supposed confusion, but Kalem saw in his eyes the knowing, the secret that he was not privy to. His father had many secrets that he held close to his chest.

'Is it true that we're going to war with the Tuki?' Kalem asked, sipping from his cup of cold tea to dispel the nervousness rising in his chest.

His father's face turned serious as he leaned back into his chair. 'If the Congress of Datus is unanimous, then yes, our country is going to war.'

'What about the other vote? Is it unanimous, father? We can't let him get away for what he did to the Payapas.'

His father looked at Kalem in the eyes, the affable parent gone, replaced by the Obsidian Datu. He waved away the room servant, who ducked out the door. It still wasn't confirmed that it was the king who had killed off an entire House, but the way the massacre was done, the method that was used, the residue of magic left behind, and the message it sent—it couldn't have been anyone else. The same had been done to House Talim more than two decades ago.

'It is enough to turn the tide, but it's delicate. If it pushes through, we throw the country into chaos, making us vulnerable to the Tuki. If the king doesn't cooperate, then the Tuki will be going into a country that has destroyed itself from within. But this may be the only chance we get to take down the king. Only chaos creates opportunities.'

'So that's a sure thing then? No matter what, the Tuki will be going to war against a country that has weakened itself from within?'

'Not necessarily. We have allies. If all goes well at the vote, we'll have a much more united country defending us against threats from within and without.'

'Why do this now, Father? Can't it wait till after we win against the Tuki?'

'I am dying. Soon. When the time comes, the south will not rally behind Duma the Jealous, who has time and time again favored the northern lords over us in all things, and who has imposed taxes and has taken major resources from our lands without giving back anything in return.'

'And you think Najima Malik of Asinar, Stark Natera of Olimawi, or even Panganay Layag of Maragtas Isles will back me when you're gone?'

'No, no, they won't, but it will be a choice between my son and the sitting king.'

Kalem narrowed his eyes at his father, trying to figure out what he meant. Datu Patas Laya of Maylaya was never known to be a cryptic man. Who he was and what he believed in had never wavered for as long as Kalem had been alive. His father was a man of war, the hero of the Obsidian Sea in the war against the Yumbani. He was a warrior before a king, but he was a good king. But over the years, as the seedsickness ravaged his mind and body, he mellowed and chose quieter, calmer battles. So he always said outright what he needed to say. Did what needed to be done. All for the good of his people.

How could his father ever think that Kalem could ever live up to his legacy? He didn't even understand why he was being asked to vote to weaken his country in a time of war.

Kalem's father must have seen the question brewing in his son's eyes. 'What is the point of a country if we let any invader take it by word or by force because the roots are rotten?' His father rubbed his index finger and thumb on his forehead, grimacing with pain. 'A broken body heals itself. It doesn't let another reap only the parts that are good.'

One of the hallmarks of his father's character was the ability to adjust himself to whomever he was dealing with. Kalem wondered how his father adjusted himself for his wayward son. 'Son, the coming years will not be kind to our balangay, and it's my fault. I had no choice in the Obsidian War.' He gave Kalem a grave look.

'I don't understand. Isn't that a good thing that the war was won because of you?'

'That's the problem. It shouldn't have been because of *me*.'

Kalem watched his father press the lip of the goblet to his lips, thinking and gnawing at words that he could not say out loud for some unknowable reason. Kalem had read every text he'd found about the Obsidian War, about how his father expertly flew a Dalaket ship over the Obsidian Sea, throwing bombs and cannons alike at enemy ships below. Historians say he was among the warrior mages in the Black Storm, leaping off the Himpapawid fleet to charge at the coming enemies, keeping them at bay, keeping them well away from the borders of Kayumalon.

Some say he landed with his veins lit red, lithe and fast like lighting, cutting down enemies left and right with kris sword and daga. Some claim that he was violet then, swinging from mast to mast, killing every enemy within his sword's reach. And then some say he landed as orange, blasting through wooden ships and sinking them to the bottom of the sea. Whatever name the sea was called before he came, nobody used it anymore. The black ships he sunk that day painted the waters. It had become an obsidian sea, it had become the Obsidian Sea.

His father would neither talk about the war nor confirm or deny any of these claims. He left home a boy prince desperate to protect his home. He returned a changed man.

His father went into the annals of Kayumalon's history as the greatest warrior mage in recent memory. All this had happened before Kalem was born.

'It was a mistake to win the Obsidian War,' his father said, but if his father had not fought, the Yumban would have landed on Maylaya way before the Imperial fleet could . . .

'The king thinks you're a threat to his reign, doesn't he, Father? Now that the Payapas are gone,' Kalem said but didn't add the last part of that thought: *therefore the king sees me as a threat and will likely want me dead before my father is gone.* 'The south rallies behind you, even Maragtas Lands. If you call for war against the Tuki, the south will follow your lead and the Dalaket will be beholden to you. They will give you what you want at Congress. The king will be forced to step down.' He met his father's eyes, face contorted into a frown, 'Why would the king purposely tear apart his own country?'

'Desperate men have nothing to lose. Chaos breaks society down to incohesive parts and pieces waiting for another hand to rebuild it. Whatever is coming, Berdugo rebels, Tuki invaders, civil war, Kalem, we won't come out of it unscathed. We have enemies on all fronts, some even closer to home, waiting to take us out of the game. The choice is either to do our duty and be the masters of our fate or do nothing and let the world decide what becomes of us.'

'Father, I'm not ready.'

The Datu looked at Kalem like he was still the boy asking for dessert before dinner.

'Have I ever told you what my own father said when I told him I wanted to travel the world on a Dalaket ship?'

'You wanted to fly ships?'

His father smiled and nodded. 'Oh yes. You see, your grandmother, my mother, Princess Diwa she loved stories, and she told me all the stories she collected from her travels. Of course, the seedsickness came, and she settled down with my father.' He sighed and shook his head at the good memory. 'I knew that I'd never live up to my father's expectations, no matter what I did. All I wanted was to see what was beyond our borders, you know? Create my own stories like her.'

'Why didn't you? What did *lolo* say?'

'He said, "Men like us aren't afforded the luxury of pursuing our dreams, not with the weight of duty bearing down our shoulders. Leave or stay, our people's blood will be on our hands." Kalem, I wish I could give you the life you want, but duty tells me that I can't. I shouldn't. I wouldn't. Either I fail you as your father or I fail you and thousands of others as Datu.'

'I don't know if I could do what you do. I . . . I chose to become a germachemist, Father, for you, *because* of you and Mother.'

'I know, son. I know. I'm sorry that you felt that you had to save me, but this is where my life has taken me.' He picked up the Obsidian Blade and placed it on the table between them. 'This is where I end and where I hope you begin.'

Kalem bit the inside of his cheek and turned away from his father, eyes desperate to look at anything else in the room—the grey walls, the wood and mahogany furniture, and the food of varying colours—until finally settling on the moons in the sky. Kalem wasn't religious or superstitious—he was an atheist after all, but all the same, he wondered how skyreaders would interpret this night sky, the subtle differences in the stars and moons and the Morningstar of yesterday, today, and tomorrow. Did they divine this moment, this part of his life, a transition and transference between two lives?

'Try for me, son.'

Kalem wanted so much for his father to understand his doubts and desperation to be who he wanted to be. It was no small comfort to know that his father had doubts, too, that he thought he had failed Kalem as a father. Now, here he was, expressing the same doubts his father had before he took the mantle, and the look on his face, expecting, loving, understanding, was enough for Kalem to make a decision.

Kalem nodded, picking up a sweet mango rice cake his father had placed on his plate and popping it into his mouth—purposely ignoring the sword between them. He would pick that up when he was ready. Mango sugar melted on his tongue and went smoothly down his throat like sweet spring water. His father poured yellow wine into both of their cups, and they both drank to their health.

His father needed him, and neither father nor son had the luxury of time. The Obsidian Sword drew an arbitrary line between them. This was where the Obsidian Datu ended and where Kalem began.

# Chapter 15

## Yin

Yin only had preconceived notions of what a Dayo fiesta was like. She had never been to one, much less been invited by a boy to go to one—a very beautiful boy at that. She imagined food and drink that were usually barred for the Dayo.

She had never taken into account the music and the dancing. It was loud in the plaza—the music becoming an indecipherable mix of the laughing and the talking and the shouting. The petals from the giant tree that created a canopy over the plaza were trampled under numerous feet. She had not imagined the smoke from the cigars, creating a cloud of colour above their heads and under the tree's branches. She had not imagined the abundance of not just food but also wine.

Tiyago took her hand as he led her into the centre of the plaza, closer to the Dayo their age. They recognized her. They greeted her. They offered her drinks and cigars. But they were wary of her. They kept their guard up around her.

Tiyago didn't notice till he returned from getting them drinks just how uncomfortable her presence made his friends feel.

He offered her two bottles of drink, one sparkling yellow, the other blue. 'What are you having?'

Yin had never had wine before, unless she counted that drop of Charmer's wine she had barely tasted that first time on the beach with Tiyago's friends, so she wasn't sure how the wines were different.

He saw the question in her face as she glanced between the blue and yellow. 'My father has never let me have wine. I don't know the difference.'

'These are like watered-down seedshooters, so the wines have some magic, but not enough that we become mages. Just a light buzz.' He raised the yellow. 'If you remember, this is Charmer's wine. It makes you feel . . . well, good.' Then he raised the blue. 'This is the Soother's wine. It relaxes you. It helps you sleep.'

Yin didn't need help sleeping. In fact, she shouldn't let her guard down right now, not around these people, not when her father was nowhere in sight. And with the Reds prowling along the outskirts of the plaza, she didn't want to fall into a false sense of security here. 'I guess I want the yellow.'

'Oh good. Only the elders drink the blues,' he said, taking a swig from the bottle before handing it to her and leaving the blue on a random table. Upon his urging, she drank, too, and the buzz was instant, like a thousand voices talking at the same time in her head.

'I take it that this is your first harvest fiesta with other Dayo?'

'This is my first fiesta ever. My father never let me go in all the other places we've lived in. I'm not allowed to go out much.'

'Didn't you say you were from Maylaya?'

'I came from Maylaya before we settled here, but I've been to other places.'

'So, you weren't born in Maylaya? I had a feeling.'

'How did you know?'

'Your accent,' he said. He took the bottle from her to drink again, which only made her want to take another swig. He was right. It made her feel good. Every drink gave her a prickling feeling running underneath her skin, and the buzzing had become a soothing note in the back of her mind. 'But where were you born really?'

She shrugged. 'I suppose it's Maylakanon. It's the place in my earliest memory.'

'Oh! So you're a city-born Dayo. No wonder your accent is gone.'

'But what about you? Are you originally from here?'

He nodded, his eyes darting around the place, a commotion somewhere on the other side of the plaza distracting him momentarily. 'Born and raised. I was sent to work in Castel before. I had to live there for half a year. Best year of my life.'

'Why? What kind of work?'

'Just labourer stuff. Whatever the masters needed. But that's not the best part. Castel is amazing! Dayo in Castel are allowed to learn other trades. I learnt how to read and write. I met thinkers and statesmen and scholars and seedmages. They didn't care that I was Dayo. They only cared about my work. It wasn't a perfect city, but it was better than a plantation. You should go there if you can. I know I would go back there if I got the chance.'

'Why didn't you stay?'

'I'm not exactly free, am I?' He said, like he was reminding her what he was, but it wasn't said with spite. Only with an odd sense of loss.

'Sorry,' she said, casting her gaze down sheepishly.

He lifted her chin up, so she was looking at him. 'Hey, hey, it's not your fault, Yin,' he said kindly. 'I am optimistic, though, that those thinkers and scholars can change the world in my lifetime.'

'Maybe you don't have to wait,' Yin said, trying to sound hopeful. 'Of all the plantations I've been to, this island had the least restrictions on Dayo. Maybe it's already starting here.'

He smiled, and it was the same smile he wore the first time she had seen him from the Dalaket ship coming here. 'There was one student scholar from the Alaala Archives. He was the son of a Datu. He advocated for equality among all Kayuman. And he didn't just mean between the Kayuman and the strangelords, but all of the people living in Kayumalon. He included the Dayo. He included people like us! He dared call us Kayuman like everyone else. Imagine a future where the colour of your skin doesn't matter?' Yin could tell that he wanted to say more, but his frown directed to someone behind her indicated that he wouldn't, couldn't. She looked over her shoulder and saw Rejeena, surrounded by a posse of her friends.

'Is he prattling about his trip to Castel again?' She said, smirking, looking at the boy holding her possessively by the waist like he owned her—a different person from the one

Yin saw at the beach. 'Don't let the Reds catch you talking shit. You remember what happened to your brother.'

Tiyago glared at the girl, but he took Yin's hand. 'Let's go, Yin.'

Yin looked over her shoulder as Tiyago dragged her to a different part of the plaza. 'I don't understand. Did something happen to Feri again?'

'Feri is fine,' he said, settling in a less-crowded part of the plaza on the sidelines. 'She meant my older brother. We were both sent to Castel. He . . .' Tiyago trailed off, seemingly surprised by how much he had said to Yin. 'It doesn't matter. It's the yellow making my tongue loose.'

'Tell me anyway.' Tiyago looked at her warily, and she couldn't deny that she knew why he was suspicious. She closed both hands around his and said, 'If it's about my father, he doesn't have to know.'

Tiyago explained after much thought. 'My brother ran away to join the Dayo Berdugo rebels in Castel.'

That was the last answer that Yin had expected. She didn't know that there were Dayo rebels. 'Rebels?'

'You didn't think that all that talk of freedom and equality wouldn't make some Dayo think, did you?' He didn't say this out of spite, and Yin was beginning to learn that Tiyago wasn't the kind to spite others for what they didn't know. So far, he had only exhibited tolerance and acceptance and patience, with her, with his friends, with Rejeena, even with the Reds. He was pragmatic, but he was also a pacifist. And the realization made her feel more comfortable around him.

They stayed like that, staring at each other, smiling, comfortable in this shared quiet space until his eyes shifted from joy to comfort to confusion and then, finally, another realization. 'Yin . . . your skin . . .'

'What?' She raised her arms up in front of her. It was faint at first, barely visible in the harsh light of the plaza, but one good look was all it took for her to see the hard glowing lines underneath her pale skin.

'You *are* a seedmage,' he said, like it was a confirmation of a suspicion he'd had, looking around them to check if anyone else had noticed. 'It must be from the wine.' He pulled her away from the plaza, backing them slowly into the shadowy sidelines till they were out of sight from everyone. 'We have to get you out of here.'

'Why?'

'Dayo aren't allowed to be seedmages,' he said, taking her hand and leading her through narrow streets and ducking into dark alleys whenever he sighted Reds.

'I don't understand.'

'Dayo are allowed to have children with Kayuman but only if the child didn't inherit the magic from their Kayuman parent.'

'I don't think that's something they can control.'

'You think that's ever stopped them?'

# Chapter 16

## Yin

Yin's skin didn't go back to normal until close to midnight. But even then, her veins were still faintly stained yellow. Her skin was just too pale to hide the residue of magic. The buzzing from the seedwine had dissipated, but there was still that slight tremor echoing in the back of her neck.

Yin and Tiyago's escape from roaming Reds—there were so many that they wondered why the Reds hadn't noticed Yin's glowing skin—led them to the far side of the village, close to the mountain pass leading up to Yin's usual haunt. Yin reluctantly led Tiyago there.

'No one else knows how to get here but me,' she said, leading them up the familiar pathway she had trudged along so many times that getting there was more instinct than memory.

She slumped at the base of the atis tree, trying to catch her breath, her fading veins adding to the moonslight that illuminated the clearing. Tiyago stayed on his feet, listening for the telltale sounds of Red troops and waiting, waiting, waiting for intruders that Yin was pretty sure wouldn't come.

'Sit down, Tiyago,' she said, leaning back into the tree. 'No one will find us here.'

'I thought I heard something.' He gave her a sideways glance, examined the field, and then crouched next to her with a sigh, still panting slightly. 'I've never seen this many Reds on the island. Something's happening. I have a bad feeling about this.'

'Should we go back?' Yin asked, raising her arms in the light to check the stains. 'I think the stains are fading.'

He gave her a good long look. 'I can still see it. You're much too pale to hide the yellow.' He held on to her wrist, looking over her pale forearms. 'Didn't you know?'

'That I had magic? Of course not.'

'You must have suspected that your father had some form of magic. It's not something Dayo skin can hide.'

That gave Yin pause. Did her father have magic? Was he a Kayuman seedmage like her? She had seen her father use seedshooters before, but he used the indigo as medicine to cure wounds, not wield magic. She looked at Tiyago's expectant face. 'I don't think my father has magic. If he did, he wouldn't be working on a plantation, would he?'

'And yet you're here, Yin,' he said, allowing the doubt to sit there, live there, fester there in her heart.

There was no sensible answer to that. At least no answer that wouldn't reveal her and her father's secret. She should have at least suspected that something was wrong in her life, but maybe she chose to ignore it as she fled from town to town. 'What now?'

'Go back to the village to check on my family,' he said, looking at her and her stained veins as if to say that he couldn't leave her here alone to do that.

'I'll be fine, Tiyago. Go to your family,' she said, despite her better judgement.

He hesitated, gazing at her like he genuinely cared about her. 'If they catch you, they won't hesitate to kill you. You know that, right?'

'That's why they won't catch me. I know this mountain better than anyone,' she said, trying to hide the trembling in the base of her throat, because if she were being honest with herself, she was terrified of being left alone. She hadn't seen her father all day. She had just found out that she had magic. If the Reds found out, they would kill her on sight.

He let out a deep breath, glancing at her and their surroundings. 'I'll come back for you. When I'm sure it's safe,' he said, standing up and pulling out a small knife from inside his shirt. He offered her the hilt. 'Take this.'

She shook her head. 'No! I don't need that. I'll just be here.'

'I'd be more comfortable leaving if you had a weapon.'

'I have a weapon.' She pointed at the black dagger stabbing the other side of the tree's trunk.

He nodded, reluctant still. He was about to run when he stopped and got down on one knee in front of her. 'This wasn't how I pictured this night.' Then he took her cheeks in his hands and pulled her into a kiss. When he pulled away, Yin exhaled, feeling lighter than she had in a long time.

'Stay here. I'll come back for you—'

A sharp, shrill, petty voice echoed in the clearing. 'Oh, you will, will you?'

# Chapter 17

## Dakila

*Six Years Ago*

It took Dakila a long time to learn that truth delayed doesn't necessarily mean a lie.

That night, when his brother Dangal blurted out that what had happened to Caritas was Dakila's fault, had engraved itself as a wound in his mind. It ate Dakila up for weeks after that, clawing at him whenever he had something to say to his father, whenever his new ageing, portly Dayo nursemaid, Lavinya, forced him to eat one thing when he wanted something else, whenever he wanted anything. He held himself back for years, afraid that he'd make the same mistake again.

But his years at Kolehiyo gave him some leeway, some room to find out what he truly wanted, to pursue his passions. And he experimented with this newfound power, this agency, over the decisions that affected his life. At the end of six years, when everyone expected him to go home and learn the ways of the court, he decided that he would enlist into the Kalasag Corps instead. He wasn't entirely sure when he'd made this decision, if it was during his Kolehiyo years or in the aftermath. He just knew that when he did make the decision, he also decided to go home to inform his father of the same. He remembered the way his father looked at him when he called him a weakling, like he was a joke, a fool in this theatre of ridicule that his father has made of his life.

Dakila remembered standing in the room. The way his father's eyes, lifting from the documents strewn across his table, had filled him with such terror that he had only managed to squeak a greeting. After Dakila had informed his father of his decision to join the Kalasag Corps, he had waited in trepidation while his father looked him over. He stared at his youngest son as if he was seeing him for the first time, and perhaps he was. King Duma was the kind of man who kept everything and everybody at arm's length. Or maybe it was the other way around. He was a suspicious man, a jealous man. Anyone who had ever tried to stand in his path had come out of it broken. His mother. Dangal. Now him. They were each shadows of the people they once were.

The corner of his father's lips had lifted and a surprised, almost amused look glinted in his eyes. He took his time looking over his son as if he was trying to find the remnants of the boy who used to cry in his mother's room.

'I didn't know you had it in you, boy,' he said simply, and then dismissed him with a nonchalant flick of the wrist. 'Come back after you've won a few wars.'

A scoff came from the doorway, echoing around the room. Stunned, Dakila turned to see Dangal standing there in black trousers and a gold-trimmed, embroidered jacket over a white tunic shirt. Their House colours hung as a sash over his shoulder and wrapped around his waist. His older brother looked every part the prince that he was, but the blank, tired aura that hung heavily about him betrayed how he actually felt. There was a weary resignation in the way he walked into the room to lay down more documents, in the way he tilted his head downward so that he was looking up at everyone, in the way he spoke, tinged with anger and distrust despite the wry smile on his face. 'You speak of wars, Father, when you have not fought in one yourself.'

'And neither have you,' his father said, tone venomous, eyes glaring daggers at his son.

'But I am not a king, and neither was the Obsidian Datu. Walk me to the main hall, *ading*,' Dangal said, finally acknowledging Dakila. 'Let us leave our father to his own devices.'

Before the king could stop them, Dangal had already taken Dakila's arm and was pulling him out the door and toward the inner courtyard garden. Dakila's aide trailed behind them as they walked.

'You look well, brother,' Dangal said, hands clasped behind his back.

Dakila maintained a distance between them, as if he might catch fire if he closed the gap. The gnawing guilt had taken hold of him again, and the words failed to come.

'I didn't hear much from you while you were at school,' Dangal said.

The tension between them was so palpable that a knife could cut through it. It was true. Dakila had not tried to reach out to his brother since he had left for Kolehiyo, had not tried to meet him in person whenever he was in Castel. He couldn't think of his brother without the guilt creeping up the back of his mind and rendering him a helpless, immobile child, just like the boy who used to cry by his screaming mother. He hadn't known how he would react to meeting his brother in person, and a big part of him was afraid of finding out.

'I wasn't sure you'd want to hear from me, *kuya*,' he said, honestly.

'I can't say I don't know why.' Dangal sighed.

Dakila gave him a quick sideways glance. 'Father has kept you busy?'

'Busy enough. I am learning to become king, I suppose. At least I am fulfilling my duty. Is enlisting into the Kalasag really what you want to do?'

'I don't want to be weak.'

His brother looked at him intently. Patient and knowing, waiting for him to finish that thought. *But it isn't what I want.* However, Dakila refused to voice this. Noting his brother's silence, Dangal nodded and pushed forward.

'Well, at least you know what you *don't* want. Most can't even articulate that.'

'It doesn't mean I know what I want.'

'No . . . No, it doesn't,' Dangal said, looking a bit more relaxed. 'At least the Kalasag will be something that's completely yours.'

*At least. At least. At least.* When did his brother begin to care about the least of things?

'Are you happy here, Dangal?'

Dangal and Dakila stopped under an atis tree and Dakila turned to face his brother, who was smiling at him sadly.

'I try to find joy in the little things.'

It took Dakila too long to understand that wasn't the same as being happy.

Dangal started up the path again. 'You should know that I don't blame you, Kila.'

Dakila followed his slow pace. Some part of Dakila told him that his brother was lying. 'Have you found her?'

A beat, drawn out like spun sugar. It was enough to know that his brother was still looking for her—if he hadn't already found her.

'Does Father know?'

'I'm sure he does. It doesn't matter. He needs me more than I need him.'

'So why stay here?'

Dangal took his time answering as they walked around a bend that circled back to the main door. 'Our father is a vile, petty, rigid man. Without an heir, he is weak. He keeps me around to stay in power. I stay to keep the few things that give me joy safe from him.' He stopped when his aide opened a door for him, then turned to Dakila and drew him into a tight embrace. He held on to Dakila with the same fierce affection he'd held the mud-streaked boy crying in Maragtas Gallery. 'I hope you send me letters this time wherever you're going, brother.'

Dakila pulled away. 'I will,' he said, though he was not sure if that was a promise he would keep.

# Chapter 18

## Dakila

*The Day Before the Congressional Vote*

Dakila hated it when things didn't go according to plan, but he hated lying to Maralita more.

Everything in its proper place. Everything where it needed to be. Everything perfect.

He stood in the corner of the park, the garrison within view. The park was still teeming with people, though the festival itself ended at midnight. Dakila was wearing a nondescript, long-sleeved black shirt, black trousers, and military-grade black sandal boots that were issued only to Dayo labourers and the lowest-ranking soldiers. He had bought a tattered black hooded cloak from a beggar, and he wore it over his head to hide the tattoos on his face and neck. He blended well enough into the crowd that he was hiding in plain sight.

He had much to hide, that was true, but not all secrets carried the shame he was feeling. He was a military officer in the Kayumalon forces, for god's sake. He had worked hard to earn his rank, and this was something no one could take away from him, not the gods, not even fate. But here he was, sneaking into the garrison like some common thief.

He avoided the main thoroughfares and cut across the Dalaket neighborhoods of Kold with their tree-lined lanes and muddy streets—most other districts had already adapted to cobblestone streets—making sure to stick to quiet side-streets and alleys to avoid prying eyes. He stopped two streets away from Magiting Garrison, in the corner nearer to the Tatsulok district where he had first found his brother's secret lodgings. He hadn't lived in the garrison for years since his promotion, but he came here often when he was on the island. The garrison itself was a horizontal stronghold the size of one small district. It housed about a thousand soldiers at any given time, more if nobles and Datus from the ten kingdoms brought their own contingents. It could get especially crowded during Reaping Festivals and during the time when sessions of the Congress of Datus were held, which was after the festival was over.

All six gates and four corners had guard towers, assigned with ten soldiers each on rotation every three hours. Soldiers who participated in the duels would likely go through the northern gate, which was closest to the arena. The two eastern gates were the busiest and the most heavily guarded of the entire fortress. Soldiers going to and from their posts around the city came through here. The western gate looked out into the harbour facing the Kayumalon Sea. The Mandaragat and Himpapawid Fleet were harboured there. The southern gate faced Tatsulok and was almost never opened. That was his entry point.

He took out a seedshooter from his pocket. He had brought three tonight, though he would probably only need one if he managed to get in and out unseen. The magic itself stained the veins, which lasted one or two hours depending on the frequency and intensity of use. He uncorked the bottle and drained its contents. The magic surged through his body, rushing so smoothly, so powerfully, like a river that knew the pathways it carved in the earth. He closed his eyes, gauging the amount of magic that this seedshooter was granting him. It rarely varied, but it was prudent to check. Many had plummeted to their deaths after running out of red seedmagic at the peak of a seed-enhanced jump.

Dakila summoned the magic dormant in his body, making his veins glow the colour of his chosen seed power, green this time, the Lightbringer seed, sending invisible mists outwards to manipulate the optical nerves, his and of those near him. The magic allowed him to create illusions, but on covert missions like this, he'd use it to make himself blend into the background, practically invisible.

He still had to stay in the shadows as he walked up to the southern gate. The magic only took effect on those who inhaled his mist. He sent out an illusion in the Tatsulok street facing the gates. In drawing illusions, he had to have the image clear in his head, ideally someone he had interacted with whom he made his illusions copy. He imagined the old man he met at Temple almost a week ago. The two guards on the ground saw it and rushed over to see what the illusion was up to while the guards on the tower above watched the surrounding area. Dakila ran forward, the green magic still cloaking him, and prepared to switch to violet to shapeshift and then to red to enhance his speed and agility. It happened in just a few short seconds, but it was enough to sneak past the guards in the tower and the guards returning from the Tatsulok border. The only downside in using seedmagic was the scent that emanated from the skin after every use. It was an immediate giveaway, so he summoned blue and indigo this time, the scent of wine and medicine similar to the ones used in the camp, to mask the other magic. It was wasteful to use blue and indigo this way, but he wouldn't have use for calming blue or healing indigo in this mission. At least, he hoped he wouldn't.

He switched back to green as he ran to hide behind the nearest barracks. His target should be in the basement of the main building in the very centre of the garrison—which was five blocks of barracks each on the two sides away from the south gate. He prepared to switch to violet, stretching his arms up the roof of the nearest barrack on the left and then switching back to red to jump, supporting the recoiling muscles in his arms as he shot up onto the roof. He landed with a soft thud and immediately switched back to green, lying flat on his stomach on top of the roof. He cursed under his breath for this gaffe and blamed a lack of practice for the amateur mistake. He readied himself to do the same thing over again, rolling down the side of the barracks in green, switching to violet to shoot out an arm toward the next roof, red to jump on top, and then green again to hide.

He looked to the side where he was supposed to land and saw a group of soldiers gathered around a fire, roasting fish they had caught in the harbor, which, thankfully, masked the scent of his magic.

This was how he had first met Maralita three years ago, as he was scouting for new recruits for his unit.

He shook the memory out of his mind and heaved himself up into a crouching position, running to the other end of the barrack, switching to red to leap forward and then to green again as he crested the peak, and then to red to land softly on the roof across. He did the process three more times and then ran to hide in a cleft in the wall at the base of the western gate. Blazing green magic, he expanded the perimeter of the mist, the scent reminiscent of sour guava thicker in the air, but it was only for a few seconds, enough for him to run across the open road that connected the eastern gate to the west.

Finally, he got to the back of the main building, just behind the grandstand and under the western tower gates. He crouched in the shadow of the tower and lit up indigo, faintly, partly to hide the scent of magic and mostly to mitigate the exhaustion. He was panting and sweat had soaked through his shirt. He tightened the cloak around him and pulled the hood down to hide his glowing veins.

Two guards were at the back door of the building. Two other guards were coming in from the barracks to replace the ones at the gates. He was pleased with himself for getting there earlier than expected.

'You there, identify yourself!'

Dakila jumped back, startled. The call had alerted the guards who were leaving the tower and those replacing them. The two at the back door stayed where they were, though they'd now drawn their curved panabat swords.

Dakila, in turn, drew the dagger hanging from his belt and ran toward the back door, preparing to force his way in.

He sent out clouds of green mist, forming into illusions of himself, mimicking his every move as he ran. Confused guards came after him, slashing at random illusions and stumbling forward when they hit air. He clicked his tongue and made a mental note to propose to the garrison commander that they should assign at least one seedmage for every two gates of the garrison.

The two guards from the gates got to him first, one slashing his blade from below, the other from above. Dakila parried the one from above with his dagger, turned and twisted just in time to avoid the one from below, allowing him to grab the man's wrist and slam the hilt of his dagger to the back of the first man's head. He punched the second man in the face. The second group from the barracks and the first man who found him joined the fray, ignoring his illusions. One grabbed his dagger hand, and the other stabbed forward, barely missing Dakila's chest. The third aimed at his head. Dakila turned off the green and woke up orange, turning muscle into stone, bone into metal. He accepted the blade on hardened shoulders, creating a slight dent there, then elbowed the second man and wrenched himself free of the first. Dagger still in hand he threw it at the third man who had cut him on the shoulder—hitting him square in the eye—threw an uppercut at the third and pushed forward the second.

He stepped back from the bodies sprawled on the ground and was met with only one guard at the door. The other was running to get reinforcements. He sighed and switched to violet, shooting one limb toward the fleeing man while also running towards the guard who had remained at the door. The violet ran out just in time that the arm recoiled, unexpectedly setting the momentum and slamming two guards against each other, knocking them unconscious.

He turned around to see the mess he'd made and sighed again. So much for sneaking in unseen. He closed his eyes and felt for the magic surging through his veins. Checking the seed reserves in a body's system was akin to checking how fast or how slow blood was flowing in and out of the heart. Which is to say, extremely difficult. Violet was out and so were green and orange. Orange was a one-use seed after all. There were some red left, though not enough to get him out of the garrison. Indigo was running low, and he remembered the dent on his shoulder, which was bleeding profusely now that it was back to flesh, soaking his shirt in blood. He drained the last of the indigo to heal himself. All that was left was blue and yellow, none were of much use in a fight. He reluctantly popped open another seedshooter and drank. He was going to feel withdrawal after this, not to mention the vein-stains would stay longer than he had originally planned for. How was he going to explain this to Maralita?

That was a problem for later.

Dakila rushed into the doorway, lighting up green and rendering himself invisible to those inside; green mist in dark, close quarters was always most effective.

He stopped at the end of a hall where the flight of stairs forked on either side of him. On the right was the holding area for witnesses, and the one on the left was for prisoners. He took the one on the right, wandered around in the darkness—his green illusions up long enough to trick those he'd passed—through the big open space scattered with random pieces of rattan furniture, searching for a familiar face among the people of all races sleeping on banig mats on the floor or huddled together around rattan chairs and tables. Finding no one he knew there, he went back up the fork and took the staircase on the left.

It wasn't long till he found himself in the basement, right at the base of the stairs. He turned off the green and used blue this time, to mask the scent of magic and blood wafting from him.

Many of the prisoners in the cages were Asinari, Asuwan, and Dayo. There was one Tikbalang, and a group of drunk Kayuman Kolehiyo students. It was crowded today, as was expected of festival weekends. There was a Dayo girl there too. The girl wasn't a streetwalker he knew that for sure, but it was telling how the Red Guard and the Kayuman in general treated the Dayo even when they were innocent. He walked all the way to the end and found the prisoner he was looking for. She wore a halter dress held up by thin twine around her neck. She had golden hair and pale skin that was red in places where she was sunburned. Dayo never got used to the Kayumalon climates, even if they were several generations apart from their winter-worn ancestors who first came to the continent. She was hugging her knees to her chest, face set in the crook between her knees, her golden hair draped over her like silk. He turned off the blue and woke the girl up by pulling her toward the bars with a violet-enhanced arm. She woke up, startled and then afraid, clutching at his wrist.

'Didn't I tell you to stay out of trouble?'

# Chapter 19

## Yin

The sharp, sinister voice echoed through the clearing. Rejeena approached them from the treeline, accompanied by a couple of their Dayo friends.

'Wait till the Reds find out about your little girlfriend's secret,' Rejeena said, eyeing them both with a malicious smile. 'You think no one noticed you glowing back there, huh, mudvein?'

'Rejeena, you don't have to do this,' Tiyago stood in front of Yin—who stayed on the ground—shielding her from Rejeena and their friends. Her companions ran over to Tiyago, overpowering and forcing him to the ground, face down, a knee on his back keeping him there. He tried to slash his small dagger at them, slicing one of them in the arm, but the other simply flicked it from his grip.

'I knew something was weird about you, girl. I knew it the moment I caught a whiff of that nauseatingly sweet stink on you,' Rejeena said, circling them, passing behind the tree and pausing to look at the dagger. 'Now I know why.' She pulled the dagger out of the trunk and pointed it at Yin as she rounded the tree. 'You think Tiyago here genuinely likes you?'

'Don't believe her, Yin,' Tiyago yelled.

Rejeena laughed. 'Did he tell you we're rewarded full freedom for every Dayo seedmage we surrender to the Reds? I would have done it myself when I saw you glowing at the fiesta, but if I made a fuss of it there, then I'd be competing with every other Dayo on the island. We don't want that, do we?'

Yin looked in horror at Tiyago, waiting for him to confirm.

'It's true,' Rejeena answered for Tiyago. 'Why do you think there are no Dayo seedmages on this island, Yin? So many halflings, and no mages? Impossible!'

'I wasn't going to turn you in, Yin,' Tiyago said.

'No, you're giving her to the rebels, right, Tiyago?'

Yin saw Tiyago's jaw clench. 'Stay away from her, Rejeena.'

'Tell me I'm wrong, Tiyago,' Rejeena said, crouching next to Yin, dagger still pointed at her. 'Tell me you didn't intend to use her,' she asked him, without turning away from Yin. 'Go ahead, girl. Ask him.'

'Is that true, Tiyago?' Yin asked.

Tiyago tried to struggle free from his captors' hold, but despite his efforts, they kept him down. 'I wasn't going to force you to go if you didn't want to.'

'So . . . it wasn't real,' Yin asked, her voice barely audible. Why did she feel an overwhelming sense of betrayal? Like she'd been naive this whole time? Like her father had been right to keep her from the world? She had hoped to belong here, to find a place to settle and be her own person. Had she been fooling herself this whole time?

Were these people among those who were after her? The ones she and her family had been running away from for as long as she remembered?

'So, who's it going to be?' Yin asked, the betrayal giving way to rage in her heart. 'The Reds or the rebels?' She tried to stand but the dagger pressed into her neck, nicking her flesh slightly, a drop of blood sliding down her skin and onto the blade's black surface. Her vision blurred, weaving in and out of reality.

The silence was still, like the world had stopped, all movement frozen in time except Yin, who looked at each of the faces, once sinister, now surprised and horrified by the sight of her. And then there was an explosion of light.

Rejeena and her companions shielded their eyes, and Tiyago ducked his head into the grass. Yin took that opportunity to grab the dagger from Rejeena's hand, attempting to loosen her death-like grip. The struggle ended up with Yin rolling in the grass with Rejeena, fighting for the weapon, the light slowly fading again. Suddenly, she was on top of Rejeena, straddling her, keeping her down, fighting her for the weapon. Rejeena slashed at her leg, surprising Yin, flipping them over, and raising the blade over her head. Yin raised her arms to shield herself and closed her eyes for the impact.

A sharp pang twisted in Yin's chest, taking all breath, all warmth, all life from her. When the light was gone, the dagger was buried in her chest, and blood spurted out of her mouth.

Rejeena tried to pry the dagger out, but it didn't budge. Her companions, their vision restored, ran from the scene, freeing Tiyago who pulled Rejeena off Yin.

Rejeena ran away too, leaving Tiyago with a dying Yin.

'I've got you,' Tiyago said, gently trying to pull the dagger out but to no avail. Instead, he pressed his palms around the wound, trying to keep the blood from running out. It was no use.

Yin was dying, she knew it. She felt the life draining out of her every moment. An entire life spent running to survive, just to end up here. The gods must have a wicked sense of humor.

'Tell me what to do, Yin!' Tiyago said, struggling, panicking over her, holding her hands, as if that was enough to hold her together.

'Go to your family,' Yin said, but the words came out breathy and barely audible.

'I won't leave you.'

'Ga—Galenya . . .'

'But . . .'

They both knew that if he left and something was indeed wrong in the village, there was no way he would be able to make it back in time to save her.

'Send Galenya . . . Father . . . Indigo . . .' she struggled to say, more to convince him that he would be more useful to her in leaving than in staying here with her as she died. 'Hurry . . .'

And that last word was what really sent him away, leaving Yin alone with the buzzing of magic in her head shifting into a singular ethereal voice.

Light burst out of her chest where the dagger was stabbed right through and reformed above her as a golden, glittering raptor.

The seedgoddess introduced itself to her before she died.

# Chapter 20

## Kalem

*A Week Ago*

'Finally ditching books for swords, eh, Kalem?' Panday said, whistling as he walked into Kalem's makeshift laboratory in the Maylaya embassy and toward the black blade on the sword stand. 'If I'm not careful, I'll be out of a job.'

Kalem saw Panday circling the blade from his periphery. He couldn't bear looking at it so he had placed it on the opposite side of the room, far from his examination table where he was working on different base metals, woods, bones, and seedmagic cocktails. After three weeks of working and studying with his father, he needed a distraction, something familiar to keep his mind occupied. 'Please. It's not like I give you a lot of work.' He cast one quick look at Panday's burn-scarred face, taking care not to look at the sword. 'Who would you be protecting me from? School bullies?'

Panday snorted. 'Speaking of school bullies, your cousin dropped by on the way to Maragtas Park.' In a matter of days, Maragtas Park would be the venue for the Reaping Festival events, including the much-awaited Sinawali Duels at the arena.

Panday stopped and leaned toward the metal to get a closer look. 'Says you were expelled and fled crying in shame.'

'Of course the snot-nosed brat said that,' Kalem said absently, as he mixed different-coloured seedshooters into a beaker. He watched the colours shift and dance and glitter within the glass container until the blend became a translucent, iridescent white that started glowing. 'For the record, I wasn't crying.' He poured a drop of the cocktail on each of the containers of metal, wood, and bone laid out in a neat row in front of him. 'And I wasn't expelled. I dropped out.' White mice squeaked in the cage at the corner of the table. 'What do you do all day then when I'm at school?'

'Oh, you know. Fun stuff. Nothing you would understand.'

'I resent that. I know how to have fun.'

Panday snorted. 'Yeah, you do, quill quack.' He met Kalem's annoyed face before turning his focus back on the sword again. 'So, are we going home soon then? To your ancestral home in Maylaya? Am I to call you "your grace" now?'

Kalem glared at Panday, who was wearing leather pants and a loose shirt thin enough that the black tattoos were visible under the fabric. Tattoos were used to indicate position, hierarchy, accolades, affiliations, and fealty among the Kayuman. The more tattoos one had, the higher they were in Kayuman society, but the tattoos themselves showed the story of the man. Panday's tattoos told the story of his fallen banner house, of how he'd been training to become a metalsmith before the fall, and of how he became the ward of the House Laya and later Kalem's aide and best friend.

'My father is still alive.'

'And you'll be a proper prince when we go back. You have your father's sword and all. When are we going home to Maylaya?'

Kalem pursed his lips into a thin line, avoiding looking at his friend and bodyguard, who had lifted the sword out of its stand.

'After the Congress.'

He focused on how the magic was reacting to different conduit materials and on the mice that were feasting on several handfuls of rice grain he'd dropped in the middle of the cage. He felt queasy remembering the gore he used to leave in the natural sciences laboratory whenever he conducted his experiments. Maybe continuing that experiment here in his father's embassy in Castel wasn't such a good idea after all.

'Beautiful blade. I've been wanting to take a closer look at this. Say what you want about the Yumbani, but they make excellent swords. They can match any Kayuman metalsmith.' The blade whistled with every swing Panday took. 'And look at the materials they used. Black living wood for the hilt, diamond pommel, and the metal—there's nothing like this in the world.'

At that Kalem looked up from his table and eyed the sword suspiciously. 'What do you mean there's nothing like it in the world? You make blades like that all the time. That's what Alagadans use in the Reaping rituals.'

Panday frowned at him as if Kalem had just insulted him. 'No, man. This thing is one of a kind. I can make metals black with chemicals and fire or maybe black plating, which is the same process that Alagadans use to make their ritual blades, but this metal was black to begin with. You don't get black blades like this naturally. Not if the gods don't send more from the Skyworld. If I didn't know any better, I'd say this was forged with arcane magic.'

Kalem's heart skipped a beat. Had he been so focused on his own studies that he closed himself up to progress? He went to Panday, took the blade and eyed it in the morningstarlight streaming through the window. He turned it this way and that, allowing light to touch every surface of it. The black wooden hilt was warm in his palm, as was expected from living wood, but this one seemed to pulse, like the sword itself had a heartbeat, and it felt like it was shifting under his own palm, adjusting to his grip. The metal was black from tip to edge; shadows disappeared on the surface, even on the debossed engravings, and light refracted around it.

He pushed aside the other materials on his examination table, many of which fell off the worktable and onto the floor (most of the non-living wood had melted from where he dropped seedmagic on them anyway, rendering them useless), and placed the sword in the newly opened space on the table.

Panday stood next to him, watching him raise the beaker of seedmagic cocktail over the blade. He looked at Panday as if asking for permission. The pinkish burn scar around his right eye deformed the eyelids so that eye was permanently squinting. Panday let his hair grow longer on that side of his face to cover the scar. His friend shrugged. 'It's a nice blade, but it's not mine. And I'll probably enjoy watching you squirm while your father yells at you for melting the sword.'

'Thanks, I guess?' Kalem poured the seedmagic cocktail on the metal and both men watched with bated breath as the iridescent liquid sat on the surface, unmoving, glowing, and unsuspecting.

And then it sizzled like water droplets on a hot pan before melting, falling into the engravings and disappearing into the metal. Kalem and Panday exchanged surprised looks.

He touched the edge of the blade and inadvertently pricked the tip of his index finger, drawing a dot of blood and sending surges of electricity down his forearm as if he'd dipped his hand in a bucket of seedshooter cocktail. His veins lit up white for a second before it was gone.

The letter engravings glowed white and then indigo, which surged right through the blade and into the pommel at the hilt. And in the back of his mind where he thought he heard voices other than his own, he heard it saying in a lost arcane language very few understood, very clearly,

***'Pierce the heart, fuse the soul.'***

Kalem startled back, looking around the room for the source of sound. There was only Panday and the mice with him. He turned to the blade and emptied the beaker on it. The pommel exploded with light that flowed into the blade, transforming it into what Kalem could only describe as liquid metal. It was the same colour as the cocktail now, white, glittering, iridescent, and transparent, like the sword itself had become glass with mist swirling inside it.

***'Pierce the heart, fuse the soul.'***

This time the voice came from the blade, echoing the same words that the voice in his head spoke. Kalem tentatively reached for the hilt, still expecting the blade to melt in his hands.

Panday grabbed Kalem's hand. 'Maybe you shouldn't?'

'Don't you hear it?'

'Hear what?'

'The voice.'

Panday cast him a concerned, knowing look. He understood what that meant. Hearing voices was a symptom of oncoming seedsickness. 'You're hearing voices now?'

Kalem looked away, suddenly feeling self-conscious. 'It's not . . . The one in my . . . The sword . . .'

'Does your father know? Does Master Makabago know?'

Kalem took his hand from Panday's grip and focused on the blade, all his theories and studies and research reforming in his mind, like a puzzle that was finally making sense after a missing piece had been found. It thrilled him, just how close he was to a very real germachemical discovery. 'It's not seedsickness.' He took out a couple of mice from the cage and put the poor creatures into a separate glass container that he hoped would minimize the . . . gore, should this experiment go badly. 'I've been studying seedsickness, trying to find a cure before . . .' Kalem trailed off as the mice frantically jumped along the sides of the container, trying to escape. 'I found mythologies about the godvessels before and after the Transference—or what the Alagadans call the Reaping. They exhibited similar episodes of mania and physiological transformations as those of my Father and Mother. They also heard voices before they were discovered, and their bodies shrunk like something in them was consuming their insides. That was as much as I could find before the headmaster caught me stealing from his private library.' He knew now that he was so close to a very real discovery. It was all finally making sense—the mythologies, the stories, the legends he's been reading in search for answers. He had simply been asking the wrong questions. He had to experience it for himself to know. This could prove just how right he was. With the desperation to confirm his theories overpowering his better judgement, Kalem picked up the sword. 'The Alagadans always used a specific blade in their Reapings. It was black like this, too. I've tried one of their blades—don't ask how I got one—and have failed disastrously every time.'

Kalem prepared to stab one mouse.

'By "disastrously", what did you mean?' Panday asked, watching Kalem carefully as if assessing the type of danger his ward was putting both of them in. 'Will it kill you? More importantly, will it kill me?'

Kalem pulled the blade back before he could kill the mouse. 'In the last experiment, all the specimens . . . exploded. This is special metal. Maybe it will go well this time.'

'You see my dilemma here, right, Kalem? You're trying to find a cure so you and your own don't die from the seedcrazies, but you're about to do something that may or may not make you go boom. If you die while I'm standing next to you, you're going to make me look bad to my next employer.'

Kalem scowled at Panday. 'You were just complaining that I wasn't giving you enough work.'

'Which in my line of profession means I'm doing a good job.'

Kalem rolled his eyes and pointed the sword at one of the mice. He turned away as he lowered the sword slowly, but a surge of energy zapped in Kalem's hand, making him drop the sword, which landed with a loud clang on the floor, blade touching his bare feet.

***'That vessel is too small.'***

Kalem looked at Panday to see if he heard that, too, but his friend only looked at him weirdly, like he was halfway between cracking a joke and scolding Kalem for trying to get himself killed. He turned to the mouse he was about to stab and said to it in his head, *'Where are you?'*

***'Are you talking to me or the mouse?'***

Kalem jumped back, his jaw nearly on the floor. He picked up the mouse and stared into its black beady eyes. *'Yes.'*

'What's happening?' Panday asked.

***'You're scaring the mouse.'***

Kalem dropped the poor creature, which scurried all over the room until it found the door. Confused, Panday scratched the back of his neck. 'Sibila won't be happy that you let loose a mouse in the house.'

Kalem ignored Panday. *'Where are you?'*

The glowing sword on the floor pulsed like a heartbeat. Kalem picked it up and stared at it. *'You're in the sword?'*

***'More like I'm only able to talk to you through a conduit. We won't need it once we've completely fused.'***

*'Completely fused?'*

***'Pierce the heart, fuse the soul.'***

'Kalem, what is happening?' Panday said, holding Kalem's shoulders and shaking him slightly. 'Is it the seedcrazies? Should I call Master Makabago?'

Kalem blinked as if he had woken from a trance, noticing just now how hard Panday's grip was on him. Dazed, he shook his head and said, 'No, no, I'm fine.' Panday pulled up a chair for Kalem to sit on. 'I'm fine,' he said again, as if trying to convince Panday that he actually was when he didn't believe it himself. 'Do you mind giving me a moment alone?'

'Not a chance,' Panday said, crouching so he was eye-level with Kalem. He looked at Panday's face, looking agitated and worried, looking like he was ready to punch a hole in the wall or throw the sword out the window. 'What happened, Kalem?'

'It was the voice, Panday. It's talking to me . . .'

'That's it.' Panday got up to leave. 'I'm getting Master Makabago.'

'No! No! It's not that. It's . . . uh . . . You know how with my father and mother, the voices are talking *at* them?' Panday raised an eyebrow. 'This voice was talking *to* me. Like we just had an actual conversation.' Kalem swept his gaze around the room and let it fall on the still-pulsing blade in his hand. 'I think it's because of this.' He raised the blade up to his chest, remembering the Reaping ceremonies. 'Pierce the heart, fuse the soul,' it had said. 'I think I'm supposed to do this . . .'

Panday grabbed Kalem's wrists, stopping him from stabbing himself in the chest. 'Do you have a death wish, you idiot? If it's the seedsickness, we can get Master Makabago to make you the seedshooter cocktail. Gods, you can even make your own!'

Kalem stared at his most loyal friend's scarred face twisting with concern Kalem had rarely seen. He remembered the first time he met Panday Talim when they were boys. The burn scar was fresh and wrapped in bandages. He'd lost his entire adopted family and his home, and he couldn't even cry because of the scar. It had taken a while for Panday to open up to anyone, and he protected those he let in with the fierceness and savagery of a cornered animal. He would not let anyone else in his life die while he watched.

'If I try this now, I might still heal my father. If I fail, then I wouldn't have to *die* because of *seedsickness,'* Kalem said, matching Panday's determined stare.

Panday wavered, his hands shaking on Kalem's wrist, his eyes flooded with so much doubt and emotion and anger.

'Please, Panday. You have to trust me. I know this is right.'

'How? How do you know it's right?'

Kalem scrambled for an answer in his mind. He's been studying this for years and read every resource he could find on the Alagadan Reaping. Many things could go wrong with this experiment, the worst of which would be him exploding like the many lab animals he'd killed by accident in school. The voice said that the vessel was too small, which to Kalem provided an explanation for the explosions. He'd been using the wrong conduit and vessel. But even if he wasn't steeped in the study of this, a part of him knew that this 'fusing' with the being, was right. 'I just know, Panday.'

Even if Kalem didn't answer, Panday understood that this was something Kalem had to do, and he would insist on doing it no matter what. He tightened his grip around Kalem's wrist and then pulled away abruptly.

'Go on then,' Panday said without looking away, determined to see this one through till the end, no matter the end.

Kalem swallowed hard and nodded slowly, raising the tip of the sword up to his chest again. He didn't notice that his breathing was shallow and fast until right then, and he forced himself to inhale and exhale deeply and slowly to calm down his raging nerves. He counted down in his head and plunged the sword straight through his chest before he got to one.

# Chapter 21

## Yin

Yin felt herself floating in a dark void, the memory of her body slipping out of her mind. Her presence was troubling, like she was scared, manic, and resigned all at once the moment before she hit the bottom, the morningstarlight barely breaking through the surface above her. She wasn't breathing, though she felt the breeze cradling her in this space. Still, she was aware that she didn't need breath here. Not here.

The Goddess flew around her in dazzling, billowing sheets of magic, forming and reforming as a great raptor she barely remembered from mythology.

***'I am Dian, the Goddess of the East Wind,'*** the Goddess introduced itself. Yin wasn't sure she could speak in this space, this consciousness, till the words were somehow articulated in the void.

*'Where am I?'* She asked impulsively. It was the least important question she should be asking, so she asked another. *'Am I dead?'* And another. *'Is this the afterlife?'*

***'Just another life,'*** the Goddess said cryptically before it flashed into an explosion of golden light, and Yin awoke with a gasp back in the real world.

She sat up abruptly, her head spinning from the sudden movement, from the memory of what happened before she passed. Her veins glowing. The skirmish with Rejeena. Tiyago running back to his family. Her father still nowhere to be found.

And the wind speaking to her in her dreams of the afterlife.

Her hand went to her chest, the dagger still buried there, but it didn't feel foreign. It didn't feel painful. In fact, it felt like it was a part of her, an extension of her body, mind, and soul. She pulled its hilt and slid it out of her body, trailing curtains of light out of her chest. She touched the part of her chest where the wound should have been. She felt no traces of the wound, not even a scar, but when she looked down at it, there was a slash of black, the width of the blade, that looked like a peephole into a night sky. She stared at the blade, raised it into the light. It had changed, like it had siphoned all its magic into Yin, leaving it a hollow crystalline dagger filled with glowing, glittering golden liquid, much like the raptor floating around her head.

Dawn was coming, and the last of the seven moons was sinking into the endless night. Still, the raptor that floated next to her seemed brighter by comparison.

'What are you?' She tried to ask, but it was gone before she could finish speaking.

How much time had passed since she . . . *died*?

So many questions swam in her head, but even with the apparent changes to her being, the more mundane questions floated above it all. What had happened to her father? Did Tiyago get to his family on time? Was there any real danger in the village?

She clipped her dagger to her belt and walked out of her safe haven to find out.

She cautiously walked into the village, barefoot, clothes shredded, and vulnerable. She wrapped her mother's scarf around her head, a vain effort to cover her face. The village was quiet, too quiet even on the day after a harvest fiesta. The doors of every Dayo household were open or broken into. Every piece of furniture, every fixture, every storefront defaced, destroyed, and demolished. And the streets were stained with dark maroon spots that she knew were blood.

She stayed in the shadows, though these were few, as the Morningstar approached the Skyworld's peak.

She skirted the plaza, careful not to be seen by the Reds standing guard there. They were just waiting, but when she looked up at the Kanlungan tree, the giant tree in the middle of the plaza, she let out a shriek in shock, her palms instantly going up to her face to cover her mouth just in time to muffle the sound. Her father was hanging by his tied hands from one of the branches of the plaza tree, which had somehow died in the night. There were other Kayuman there, many known to be allied to Dayo either by blood, by marriage, or by principle. She recognized some of them as Tiyago's halfling friends, including Rejeena, who had a big bloody slash across her neck.

Without thinking, she ran to free her father, but she was tackled into a narrow alley before she entered the plaza and was seen by the soldiers.

Tiyago pressed his palm over her mouth, his other palm pressing her hard against the wall, mouthing 'Don't. Quiet.'

He looked out the alley for danger and seeing nothing, he took her hand and dragged her deeper into the space and crouched there, waiting.

'We're safe for now. That is, until the rebels try to take back the plaza from the Reds,' he said, tucking his small knife into his belt. 'But the Reds will be patrolling these narrow streets again.' He held her shoulders, looked her from head to toe like he was searching for evidence that she was real, that she wasn't a trick of the light. 'How?'

'I woke up like this,' Yin said, purposely not mentioning the raptor. 'Galenya said that the atis tree's fruit was magic. Maybe it healed me.'

He cast her a look that said he didn't believe her, but he didn't push the topic. Not now. 'The Reds hung your father there on purpose. You didn't say he was a deserter from the king's guard.'

'I didn't know. I just knew he was a soldier before he worked in plantations.'

'I believe you, but they think he stole something very important during his service. I think they're looking for you. They're killing every female Dayo halfling they could find.'

'Me? Why me?'

'Why indeed? Who are you, Yin? Where are you really from?'

'I'm Yin. I told you where I *think* I'm from.'

'There are rumors among the Dayo in Castel . . .' He looked at her face like he was searching for answers that she was absolutely sure weren't there. Then a light in his eyes flicked on, like a lamp in the window at night, lit by a realization that Yin could not understand. 'We have to hide you until the Reds are gone.' He stood to leave and took her wrist to drag her with him, but Yin stopped him.

'Tell me what's happening,' she asserted, taking her hand back. 'I'm not following you anywhere until you explain this to me.' Her voice was louder than intended, and it echoed down the alleyway.

Tiyago shushed her and crouched next to her again, listening for incoming intruders. Nothing. For now.

'I'm not sure yet . . .' he began tentatively. 'But I think you're from the Maragtas bloodline.' He took her hand, pulled her up to stand with him, and began to walk forward quietly. 'Until we can confirm it, we have to keep you hidden and safe.'

He had spoken too soon, because in minutes, they were surrounded by Reds.

* * *

# Interlude

The Spider's palace was a gilded cage. Jin dared not let her guard down when she was in the palace where she shared a room with her *siblings*, not by blood, just other seedmages fused with gods and connected by a common master. She didn't even let her guard down at night when Jjada, the capital city, slept off the winter cold that constantly tormented it.

The room had a connecting door that opened into the Spider's chambers. Two rows of four beds each lined the walls opposite each other with a chest for their personal effects at the foot of each bed. Only six beds had occupants when there were once eight. The Spider ate the two. Their power belonged to the Spider now.

Jin took her time returning to the palace, which was a month, considering that the palace was on the opposite end of the country from the small, ruined town. Still, she felt like a month wasn't enough time for her to truly consider what she was about to do. During the entire ride back, she replayed in her head her conversation with the Shadow. *'I have nothing to lose, and you have everything to gain,'* he had told her. He was right. When the Spider was gone, Jin would regain what she had lost, what the Spider had kept locked up in her frozen dungeon; she would be able to reclaim what little freedom she had. They were both practically gods, but the Shadow had nothing to lose and Jin had everything her heart desired used against her by the Spider. If she was wrong about this, if this didn't work, she would lose everything. What was power without love? When she thought about it that way, the decision was easy to make.

Jin was not new to war. The last one against the Lastans had only been a couple of decades ago but the Spider's fury in war was not a memory that Jin would soon forget. No one knew the limit of her power. The Spider was conscientious about how and when she used the magic but she was aggressive in acquiring it. One would think that she was stockpiling power for the day she would have to fight a bigger, more powerful enemy.

But having that many gods pull her one soul a thousand different ways must have had an effect on her. The Spider barely seemed human any more.

Jin stomped through the giant double doors of the palace, determined to deliver her message of war before she lost nerve. She would be pitting an immortal, inscrutable being against the monarch of the most powerful country in the world. For better or worse, war was a deliverance of permanent change to a system, and if she did this, she would have the blood of thousands of people in her hands.

All for the love of her life.

A girl, her height barely reaching up Jin's chest, met her at the first turn and walked in stride with her. 'What did you find?' Hanabi asked, voice almost inaudible over the sound of static and lightning surging through the younger girl's veins, as they made their way to the Spider's personal quarters. Hanabi came from a ruined city on the border of Lasta and Tukikuni. She had the Lastan sharp nose and strong jaw and the Tuki almond-shaped eyes and bluish pale skin. Hanabi was a young mortal girl when the Spider came to her city at the beginning of the Lastan War and looking at the girl's worried face now and remembering the violence that she'd had to live through, Jin was reminded of her own beginnings, of the Spider coming to her own hometown. It was so long ago that the memory felt more like a dream now than an actual vision of the past.

All of them carried the weight of war, but none had repurposed it into armour as well as Hanabi had.

Jin clenched her jaw, unsure how to answer or if she should even tell the girl her news before she spoke with the Spider.

'A message,' Jin answered simply. It was better to give them the news after she's talked to the Spider.

'What kind of message?' Another girl asked, walking in step with Jin and Hanabi. Seyo was the youngest of their group, born at the tail end of Lastan War, and fused as a child barely half Jin's height. Her family, or what was left of them, were imprisoned in the Spider's ice dungeon many floors below the surface. Her power was foresight. She saw the many possibilities of the future all at once, but she could never tell which possibility became a reality until it happened before her. 'I saw shadows, Jin.'

'Shadows are everywhere, Seyo, so long as there is light,' Jin said without slowing down, trying and failing to ignore her *siblings*. They were not her siblings. They would simply be the first casualties of war.

'But this shadow had a face, a malicious smile, the scent of decay,' Seyo said.

'Perhaps it was just Gamu, coming back from smoking his weeds,' Jin said, forcing Gamu to come out in the open to walk with her to the Spider's chambers.

Gamu was a young boy in the body of a big, bulky man. The sides of his head were shaved clean of hair, flanking the row of red braids running from the top of his head down to his neck. His red beard was braided neatly and held together with a copper ring. Gamu was all Lastan, a warrior from a northern tribe that the Spider had wiped out when her defense had turned into a campaign to push forward the borders of Lasta. 'Just trying to get the edge off, big sister.'

Jin gave Gamu a sideways glance, making contact with his knowing look. Everyone had been on edge since Kayumalon won against Yumbani. It was unprecedented, but Tukikuni's war against Lasta and Kayumalon's crackdown on foreign maritime trade set off a series of events that had pushed the Yumbani to desperation—far enough that they'd dared to attack Kayumalon by sea. Rumour had it that a godvessel that had been in the possession of the Yumbani since the exodus of kings was among the spoils of war. Tukikuni had since been waiting for the repercussions.

Two other siblings were waiting at the Spider's door, casting hopeful and at the same time fearful glances at her. They all knew it was inevitable, but she empathized with her siblings. Just because their fate was inevitable didn't mean they had to put on a brave face. No matter what the Spider did with her news, it didn't change the fact of what their true purpose was here.

She felt the same way, but she knew that she was likely the one who would outlast her siblings. She'd served the Spider too well over the years. She'd worked hard, waiting for this opportunity to come. Chaos ushers in change when the status quo refuses to bend with the ever-changing times.

'It's not fair,' Hanabi said, stopping Jin from pushing open the Spider's closed door. A chilling silence fell among them.

'Glorified containers is what we are,' Gamu added with an air of hopelessness.

'Isn't there anything you can do, big sister?' Seyo asked, pulling at the hem of Jin's cloak.

Jin looked at each of their faces, all terrified and alone, and she realized how wrong the Shadow was.

She did have something to lose. The question was if her love was worth the sacrifice.

The bill came at the end, and she answered her sibling's singular question by opening the door.

# ACT 3

# Chapter 22

## Yin

Yin lived a small life. Cramped in small rooms, small houses, small hiding spots, small boats, small cages. Never having room to stretch her arms outward, to extend her legs, to breathe.

As a young girl, she remembered living in a room much smaller than their stone house. It was on the second floor of a building that always smelled like wine and food. Her mother forbade her from leaving the room without her, and even when they did, she would only take her to the tavern downstairs where a Kayuman man in a cloak waited for them at a table. He always brought something for her—a doll, a scarf, sweet kakanin, a pretty dress. That man never looked at her with regret or guilt or grief the way her father looked at her. He was always happy to see her, always glad that he could see her. Sometimes, she wished that man was her father.

They couldn't bring all those gifts when they left the city, and she never saw that man again.

Yin woke up in a windowless room so small that she couldn't stretch out her legs when she sat, or her arms sideways when she extended them. When she stood, her head would only be a hand's width away from the ceiling. The only source of light came from the gaps around the door and the floating cloud of glitter that was perpetually on the edges of her vision. She was wearing an old black rice sack long enough that it fell above her knees. Her dagger was gone.

The walls were wooden, but it felt alive to her touch, like blood flowed underneath its surface. The floor would rock every now and then, and if she pressed her ears up to the back wall, she'd hear the wind whistling. She was on a flying Dalaket ship.

***'You need to escape,'*** the Bird-Goddess said, floating next to her face.

*'If I knew how, I would have already done it,'* she snapped at it, pulling her knees close to her chest and making herself small. She recounted the events prior. The Reds overpowered her and Tiyago. 'Run! Don't let them know!' Tiyago had said, trying to put up a fight, giving her the chance to escape, but the Reds knocked him out and dragged him away. The raptor came to her as the guards came after her, and the wind rattled the ground. It did nothing more before they had captured her, bound her, and knocked her unconscious.

*'It's not like you're being helpful.'* Yin buried her face in the crook between her knees.

*'What are you anyway?'*

***'I'm the Goddess of the East Wind.'***

Yin raised her head again, glaring, coming face-to-face with the Bird-Goddess staring blankly at her.

***'I tried to leave you. Before the flying ship left the island,'*** the Bird said, with no remorse, no notice of Yin's displeasure of the goddess' confession. ***'But I couldn't. I can't stay too far away from you. It's like I'm a string tethered to you, and the farther I go, the thinner I become, the more likely I'll snap.'***

Hope rose like bile in the back of her throat, and tainted the tone of her voice, *'How far did you go?'*

***'Just a few paces outside this room.'***

*'Can you do anything else?'*

***'Like what?'*** The Bird asked, suspicious.

*'Can you get me out of here? Like unlock the door from the outside?'*

***'I can't. I'm not tangible in this realm. You can see me only because you are walking on two realms at once through our bond.'***

Yin closed her eyes and leaned against the back wall, feeling the wind on the wood outside shaking its fibers and sliding over the surface in clear, sharp tones. It calmed her, tempered her mind, knowing that the wind was just outside waiting for her. She felt a new affinity with it, like the wind was a part of her own body, detached by the wall of living wood that separated her from it.

She snapped to attention. *'If we're bonded, does that mean I can use your powers?'* She didn't wait for it to answer, stood, and faced the back wall, placing both palms on the surface. She pushed hard on the wall, her back pressing on the door.

***'Only one way to find out.'***

She imagined herself as the wind howling at a mountain, and then at a big tree, and then at a single rice stalk, bending it to her will. From the back of her throat rose a growl that escalated into a roar. The ship rocked violently then flipped over, throwing her off her feet, and she landed with a heavy thud on the wall that was opposite to where the door was.

*'What did I do?'*

**'You called the wind.'**

Yin stood up and pressed her palms on the wall again, gentler this time, as if delicately pushing thread through a loom, methodical, delicate, lithe, only the force of her fingers at work—her palms, her wrist, her arms held back. Her veins lit yellow. The wind responded to her in smaller actions, swaying the boat to and fro, so that the floor was unstable beneath her feet. She kept her hands on the wall, feeling the wind outside, feeling her body melting into the whirlwind that cradled the boat, spinning it round and round till it fell out of the whirl and swooped forward abruptly, like a stone thrown from a slingshot.

She slammed back into the wall again, the floor steady and stable again, the Bird-Goddess still in her periphery.

*'Well, that did* something. *Can you see what happened outside?'*

**'I think so. Stay here.'**

Yin scowled, about to say, *'Where else will I be?'* But the Bird had already left, taking its light with it. Only her dimming yellow veins illuminated the box. She raised her hands up to her face for a closer look. The stains were the most intense there, like all the magic she'd channeled had gathered all over her hands so that not only her veins were yellow, her pale skin itself had taken on a subtle tint of the colour. All this from pushing the wind, feeling as if she was the wind itself. She wondered then, if she could push the wind, then surely, she could pull it too, right?

She felt her stomach churn and her ears pop as the vessel rose again. The ship returned to a steady rhythm.

The Bird-Goddess returned and perched on her raised knee. ***'You made a mess of things outside. They're coming to get y—'***

The door opened behind her before the Bird could finish talking, and Yin fell backwards through the suddenly opened doorway. She stared up at two Kayuman guards staring down at her. There was a pause after the two noticed her yellow stained veins.

'Mage!' One of them yelled down the hall, while the other made a grab for her arm.

Yin slipped under and between them, running through a straight hallway lined with blue glowlamps hanging from sconces on the walls. She passed more doors, like the one in her box, on either side of her. Though she heard the thundering footsteps of the men behind her, she didn't look back. She pushed forward till she reached the balcony at the end of the hallway that overlooked the bottom of the hull. She barely stopped in time at the railing, her body hanging over and looking down at large kegs that smelled like smoke and ash and fire. She hurriedly righted herself and spotted the stairs across the balcony. She ran to the side and rounded the balcony hanging over the hull.

The two men separated, one still chasing her, the other rushing to the other side in an attempt to cut her off at the end.

Closer and closer they got to her, and she was still far from the stairway and hallway when more soldiers streamed in, screaming, 'Dayo seedmage! Dayo mage!'

'Nobody kill her!' One voice, separate from the others, commanded.

She raised both hands in front of her face, her hands clawing at the air as if about to rip apart a loosely woven tapestry. The wind answered, casting aside men to clear a path for her, some falling off the side into the bottom of the hull, others falling backwards on the floor and hallway.

The wind blew her off too, and she slipped off the balcony, falling, falling, falling until she wasn't. The wind cradled her, like in that dream of the afterlife, raising her upward all the while thrashing her body about like debris in a typhoon. It slammed her on the ceiling, and she fought in vain to stay steady, to control the wind, to force the wind to bend to her. All her efforts, however, were futile. The wind only continued to whip her about.

*'Make it stop!'* Yin yelled to the Bird-Goddess. *'Tell it to put me down!'*

The Bird stayed in her direct line of vision, trailing glittering motes in its wake. ***'Stop thrashing like fish out of water. Fish swim. Birds fly!'***

Reluctantly, Yin stopped thrashing and let herself flow with the wind, adjusting only when she would hit the wall or the ceiling—which she always did. There wasn't enough room here to fly without hurting herself.

The wind could never be confined in a closed space. The wind dies when trapped. The wind is free.

She tried to shoot forward toward the stairway, and in her rush, she barely dodged men trying to bind her, barely evaded walls that she slammed into, barely kept pace with the wind's dance, a dance she was learning for the first time.

At last, she reached the end and pushed herself forward, her body shooting upwards into the open air. The sky bloomed before her as she rose higher and higher and higher. It was exhilarating, maddening, it was unrestrained freedom.

For the first time in her life, Yin was free.

# Chapter 23

## Kalem

***'Wake up,'*** the voice in his head began. ***'It worked.'***

Kalem's eyes fluttered open and saw tendrils of indigo mist above his face. It formed the shape of a turtle flapping its fins and swimming around the space like it was underwater. Its voice wasn't the garbled mess he had first heard. It was clear, oddly sapient, and spoke an arcane language that Kalem only understood because he had studied it. It sounded both like a creature of this world and of an otherworld—ethereal, weird, and undulating with magic.

*'I see you,'* Kalem said, fascinated by the creature.

***'And I see you,'*** it said in a rather mocking way.

*'What are you?'*

***'I am not a 'what.' I'm a 'who.' I am Damu, God of Earth.'***

*'I . . . don't unders—I am Kalem.'*

His blurred vision adjusted to the person looking down at him.

'Kalem?' Panday whispered, eyes crazed. 'You're alive. Seedgods, you're alive. You idiot!' He forced Kalem to sit up, and Kalem saw the Dalaket twins, the brother bigger than the sister by at least a foot, with their purple-leafed carapace growing over their skins and the strands of vines growing out of their heads like hair. Their black-beaded eyes were fixed on Kalem.

'What happened?'

'You stabbed yourself with the sword, and it went through your chest like you were made of water. You fell to the floor, convulsed, and then stopped moving and breathing altogether.' Panday pointed at the blade, now permanently crystalline black, on the floor next to him. 'You idiot! I thought you were dead!'

Kalem touched his body as if inspecting it for signs of life, the indigo mist-turtle still swimming around his head. In the middle of his chest, there was a black, ragged line where the sword had been, swirling with dots of white light like a sky full of stars. He certainly felt alive—his pounding chest was proof of that—but at the same time, he felt different. Heavier in soul and spirit but lighter in body. Like trapped water in a cup poured into an infinite ocean.

He felt . . . infinite.

Panday stood and then helped Kalem up. 'You had me worried about my financial future, you idiot. Don't do that again!'

Kalem saw the mouse return to the room, and he grinned. It worked. The experiment worked.

'You're not out of a job yet, my friend.'

# Chapter 24

## Yin

The sky bloomed above her, and she imagined, if she could fly high enough, if she could reach far enough, she'd breach the Skygods' realm and hold light in the palm of her hand.

Time stood still for a second that felt like centuries as she reached the summit of her flight, that agonizing brief second before the fall. Her long dark hair trailed like a scarf below her, morningstarlight kissed her pale skin, her breath mingled with the wind, the wind's breath mingled with hers. This was *her* wind. *She* was the wind itself.

And then the fall. In a sudden wave of stomach-lurching panic, she fell. She tried to hold the wind, hold it like railings around a balcony overlooking a steep drop. It tossed her body around like a flotsam in the ocean. The wind whistled and howled in her ears as she fell. The glittering mist that was the Bird-God simply glided around her, a dance that changed steps every time she thought she'd figured it out. She caught glimpses of the ocean below, deep blue with silver foam shimmering on the surface, rocks that were not big enough to be islands and islands that were all rock and sand.

The wind enveloped her body in a hurricane, cushioning her fall inches before she hit the water. The wind was restless, and it answered her confusion by jetting her still upside-down body left and right. She shot upwards again, creating a crater in the water's surface below where she was supposed to fall, thrashing as if she'd dove violently into water, her arms cutting through air hard as if expecting the wind to fight back and slow her down like water would. A leg kicked to one side sent her into a loop-the-loop, suspending her upside-down in midair again. She pulled her dress back down and kicked the other leg to set herself upright, overshooting her own strength. She whirled into another loop-the-loop in the other direction. The force of an arm pushing forward sent her hurtling in that direction, only to be pulled back where her other arm pushed. Pushing, punching, kicking in every direction all at the same time kept her unbalanced, and it took her too long to realize that it was her own force that kept her unsteady.

So, she closed her eyes and let her body fall backwards into the cradle of wind around her, letting it catch her gently in its arms. This dance was no fancy routine like the ones she watched at the plaza fiesta. It was frenetic and calm at the same time. It vibrated with life; it was a million different colours all at once. She let it carry her. She trusted its direction. She allowed herself to melt into the magic so that the wind and her were one and the same, two dancers anticipating the other's move, memorizing the subtle changes of tremors and cadences in each other.

Their dance didn't require calculated finesse. Just freedom to move, to dance, to go where it wanted to go.

So Yin danced with the wind, listened to it, and let it lead her. In turn, the wind listened to her. And when she opened her eyes again, she floated among the white-foam clouds, infinity stretching above and below her from deep blues to powder blues. She drew in a cold breath, so clear, so smooth, so very free. She raised her hand to shield her eyes from the morningstarlight, but the heat on her skin was tempered by the cold mist of cloud wind. Time slowed here, its passage only noted by her beating heart, pounding in her chest, drumming between her ears. Exhilaration rushed through her veins, infused with the magic already coursing through her body. She smiled and stretched her arms outward and breathed it all in.

***'You're flying,'*** the goddess said, hovering around her in clouds of gold glitter.

*'I'm flying,'* she said, but more to herself as if she needed convincing. *'I* am *the wind.'*

*'You are the wind,'* the raptor said right before she shot forward, laughing like a child at play, flitting between clouds and rays of light, and flying across infinitely open skies with the gods.

The moons had already risen in the sky when she dove back down. She swept over the island, circling it, and saw five ships unlike any other merchant ship she'd seen before in the harbor. They all flew the red, black, and gold patterns from their main mast. The flying ship that had captured her moored with them. She watched them warily—soldiers in sleeveless red uniforms with black tattoos up and down their arms were taking sacks of grain, seeds, and crops into the hull of their ship. On the docks, the Reds snapped whips at Dayo labourers carrying this season's harvests on their backs.

Dayo women, some with bellies swelling from pregnancy, were gathered on one ship, hands tied behind their backs, huddled into a corner, guarded by soldiers with whips.

Yin's heart raced as she scanned their faces. None were old. None were Kayuman. None were Tiyago. She flew back to the village. The Kanlungan tree in the plaza was burning and trailing fingers of black smoke into the sky.

From its branches hung bodies from nooses, bodies that were burnt black. Her father was nowhere to be seen and neither was Tiyago. She saw more bodies sprawled out among the remnants of last night's fiesta—a half-eaten Lechon that dogs fought over, upturned tables covered in spilled rice, rice cakes, and vegetables and fruits, the dead bonfire's scorch marks and blood painting the dirt floor. Tears stung the corners of Yin's eyes, panic rising in the back of her throat like bile.

She lost control of the wind again and fell clumsily on the ground, searching, hoping, praying. She ran back to her house on the outskirts of the village and stopped in front of Galenya's house, horrified by the blood seeping from the gap under the door.

Yin stepped over the blood and pushed open the door. The room was ransacked as if a hurricane had come specifically into the old woman's house to break, turn over, and destroy everything in it. Dried leaves, herbs, fruits, and vegetables were strewn all over. Shards of broken jars and clay pots were scattered over the floor which was still stained with the potions that each container spilled. The hearth in the middle of the room was burnt out, and the bed was slashed and stripped open to reveal the straw inside. The sheets were stained with more blood than she remembered. Galenya was nowhere to be found.

Maybe that was a good sign. *No body meant Galenya could still be alive somewhere*, she tried to convince herself, only to be disheartened by the memory of the bodies on the plaza's floor and hanging from the tree.

She ran out of the crooked hut and towards her own house. Any hope she had left was snuffed out when she saw the burnt ruins from a distance.

'Dayo! Stop!' A deep voice commanded her, sending tremors of fear down her spine.

She ran past her house, looking over her shoulder to catch sight of the three Reds from the plaza chasing her. She made a beeline for the tree line, not looking back, not stopping, not thinking about where she was going. Only running away, moving forward, denying the truth, and crying. She'd been running all her life. It was all she had ever known.

She stumbled over an exposed root and realized that she recognized this part of the grove. She scrambled back up to her feet and found her father sitting under a tree, hand on a wound on his side, blood dripping from his nose, his ears, and the side of his lip. He had bruises all over, like he'd been beaten up all day.

'Father!' She called, kneeling in front of the man and helplessly wiping the blood off his face. Her hands trembled as she examined the wound on his side. 'Father, please wake up.' She cried into his chest, clinging to him, shaking him gently, trying to wake him. 'Please . . .'

'Yin . . .' Her father stirred awake, groaning and squirming in pain.

'Father!' Yin said, looking up at her father's face, one eye bruised shut and bleeding, face swollen, lips cracked.

'No time. Have tell you . . . Not father . . .'

'Don't speak . . .' Yin said, looking all over for a way to move him. 'Indigo, do you have indigo left at home?'

A firm hand held her down. 'No. Real father is looking for you . . .'

'What? I don't understand. *You're* my father.'

Her father who was not her father shook his head. 'Yin . . . stay hidden . . . here . . . till he finds you.'

Before she could protest, a hand pulled her shoulder back violently, making her stumble backwards on the dirt floor. Two men stood over her, the same ones who had captured her earlier.

'I recognize you. You're that Dayo seedmage,' one Red soldier said, pointing at her yellow-stained veins.

'You were supposed to be brought straight to Maylakanon,' the other said, crouching to look at her face more clearly.

A cloud of dirt was thrown at his eyes, followed by a weak scream by her father, 'Run, Yin!'

Yin took their distraction as a cue to run away, jumping a few times as she summoned the wind that wouldn't come to catch her.

*'Why isn't the wind coming?'* She screamed at the golden raptor.

***'You're thinking of yourself separate from it.'***

She imagined the wind flowing through her own veins, enveloping her, melting in her just as she melted into it. It lifted her up slowly in the next jump, only to be pulled back down again by a hand grabbing her ankle.

Both men tackled her to the ground, forcing her to lie face down on the dirt floor, her hands held behind her back.

'Let go of me!' Yin screamed, thrashing under his hold.

'Oh, oh, I'm convinced. I'm letting go now,' he said, pretending to loosen his hold on her wrist then bearing down on her harder. The other one laughed as he rummaged through his pack. The first one pulled her head up by her black hair. 'You think I'm an idiot, huh, Dayo?'

'Yes,' said a voice as coarse as sand before wood slammed into the back of her captor's head, knocking him down and off Yin.

Before Yin could even turn around to see who had saved her, a small cry of pain, coarse, sharp, and cackling, told her who it was. Galenya was already falling to her knees with a sword pierced through her chest from the back.

'Dayo scum!' The second Red said, pulling the sword free from the old woman's body just as the first Red recovered.

'Run, Yin!' Galenya said, blood pouring from her lips. 'Up the mountain . . . Hide, girl!' She fell face forward.

Yin screamed, the wind swirling around her, a gust turning into gale, into storm, into hurricane that pushed back both Reds from her. They staggered backwards, disoriented by the magic. Anger and seething hate bubbling bitterly inside, Yin pushed and pushed and pushed until both men were nowhere near her and Galenya.

The two soldiers adapted quickly, plunging their swords into the ground to hold themselves steady. No matter how much Yin pushed, they did not budge. They only waited for her to finish. *Very well then. If pushing did nothing, she shall pull,* she thought, and then pulled the wind toward her, every bit of it curling around her like armour. The two men stumbled forward, grip on their swords slipping, bodies dragged toward Yin.

She reached closed fists forward and pulled back violently, the wind responding by absorbing more of the air around her hurricane. The Reds fell into the wind, and it threw their bodies around, their mouths pried open such that even the air in their bodies was rushing to answer Yin's summons. The two men stopped thrashing and drifted in her wind like debris in a typhoon. She dropped them to the ground with a loud thud, their bodies breaking from the impact.

In her trance, she didn't realize that her wind had picked up Galenya's and her father's bodies, which were now lying in broken heaps on the ground.

She fell to her knees, arms hugging herself, head bowed, body shaking, breath shallow.

This wasn't her fault. They were dead before she lost control. The Kayuman killed them. The Kayuman stole from their harvest. The Kayuman enslaved her people. The Kayuman destroyed her home. She felt so small again, so insignificant. Her new powers couldn't even save the people she loved. She couldn't do anything to stop the carnage.

She raised her eyes up at the night sky, the moons painting the sky with the colours of war, death, deceit, and passion; impassive gods racing across Skyworld, watching, indifferent, petty. She lost her mother to disease. She lost her father to violence. She lost every place she'd come to call home. She would lose everyone she cared about, everyone she loved, and still, the gods only watched, they did nothing.

And in the back of her mind, she thought, she was a goddess now, too. She had flown their skies and ran their race.

The wind, *her* wind, raised her up, her hair and dress billowing with her magic, her heart pounding in her chest under the starry black night. If the Skygods won't do anything to save her people, then the least she could do was avenge everyone she'd lost.

# Chapter 25

## Dakila

*The First Night of the Reaping*

Funny how the right words spoken to the right person at the right time could change a person's life.

The country bumpkin waited for him in the usual tavern in Tatsulok, but he'd shed his disguise to reveal a man with a face half-melted from a long-healed burn scar, his right eye so deformed that it was perpetually squinting.

'Hello, little nephew,' the bumpkin said with a wide grin when Dakila sat across from him in a shadowed booth in the back of the tavern. He was already halfway through a bottle of yellow. It was quiet this time of day in the tavern. The Tatsulok usually didn't wake up till the Morningstar sank and gave way to nighttime.

'We're almost the same age, Panday,' Dakila said, taking the bottle and pouring himself a drink. 'And did you have to lay it on so thick at the Temple? You made me look like a pompous jerk. I go to the temple regularly.'

'Because that's what you want people to remember about you when you're trying to be sneaky-like.' Panday leaned back into his chair in his leather pants and loose, thin shirt that barely hid his tattoos. Dakila's gaze fell on the dagger sigil in the middle of his chest, the symbol of the fallen House Talim. 'Can't have a prince seen with a southern country bumpkin, can we?'

He raised an eyebrow at Panday and then rolled his eyes. 'And why would I want that?'

'It's easier to predict how people will react to you when you know how they perceive you.' Panday snatched his goblet off the table and drank. 'Temples are chock-full of people pretending to be religious, god-fearing types with not much in their heads but the constant need to appear good.' He tipped his goblet to Dakila. 'Easy to dismiss those people, which is what you need when you're wanting to be covert and such.' He pressed the cup to his lips and said before drinking, 'Your niece is alive, by the way.'

'Are you sure?'

'As sure as I am inked, I am. Had to give up one of my good swords to find her, but I'd say it was worth it.'

Dakila narrowed his eyes at his uncle disbelievingly. He'd been wrong before and had sent Dakila on wild-goose chases across the country under the guise of secret missions. Panday was stuck on the island city as long as his ward stayed in the city, but for legwork like finding information, retrieving lost things, and hiding things that should remain lost, he was a reliable man.

'Fits the description,' he said, counting each description with the fingers of his free hand. 'Pale half-Dayo girl with a Kayuman father who was a former Red. About the same age as Kalem, maybe a tad younger. And most importantly, seedmagic. Only comes from Maragtas bloodline. Powerful magic, too.'

'Have you told *Kuya* about this?'

'He has,' Dangal said, taking a chair from an empty table next to them and sitting between him and Panday. 'I'm leaving on the night of the Congress of Datus when all attention will be on the vote. I can leave without anyone noticing me.' He shot a look at Dakila as if he already knew the question his younger brother was about to ask next. 'I'm not going to Congress. I know what Patas is trying to do, and I know better than anyone that the king won't take it—whatever *it* is he plans to do to retaliate—without putting up a fight. It's just better that I stay away.'

'But what about the Congress?' Dakila blurted out.

Dangal answered as if he had been asked about what he had for breakfast. 'What about it?'

'Don't you want a say in it?' Dakila added, disbelievingly.

Panday sank into his seat and just observed the brothers.

'Datu Patas is probably the only one left brave enough to stand up to the king,' Dangal took Dakila's goblet and downed it. 'Cowards, the lot of them.'

'Too bad that merfolk queen isn't Datu,' Panday chimed in, seeming more knowledgeable about the matter than he was. 'Be interesting what she'd do in Congress, 'stead of that bumbling husband o' hers—'

Dakila interrupted the two before they veered completely off track into drunk tavern talk. 'Let's go back to the more pressing issue?' He turned to Dangal. 'Father will find it suspect that you don't go to the gathering or Congress.

You're not even sure if it's your daughter yet. Can't he go?' He pointed at Panday with his thumb.

'Nuh-uh, nephew. No can do,' Panday said, sitting up. 'If Kalem's going to any of these monkey parties, I'm gon' be there. The boy won't see no threat if it were a snake jumping at him. Both of them, father and son, geniuses and paragons, but they'd no sooner fall on their toes when you leave them on their own too long. Obsidian Datu refuses to play dirty like the lot of them at Congress. Same as his broody son.' He tipped the last of the wine into his cup, glaring at Dangal for drinking it all too fast as he did. 'Besides, my gut tells me something bad is 'bout to happen, and my gut's always right about these things.' He tipped his chin at Dangal.

'I believe you,' Dangal said. 'My father has been quiet lately. He's not taking the changes in Congress well.'

'You mean the talk of dethroning him circling around Houses?' Dakila frowned at his brother. 'That's old news.'

'Yeah, but your genius brother right here has a vendetta against the king,' said Panday, slurring the words—Dakila couldn't tell if it was acting or if he was actually drunk. 'Went on politicking around Congress, he did. Houses were more than happy to stick it to the old man. King can't be too happy about his only son right about now.'

Dakila and Dangal exchanged looks, and Dangal burst out laughing. 'You're still talking like a bumpkin, but you spew out political insight like a bannerman.'

'You'd be surprised, *Kuya*,' Dakila said. 'He just talks with a southern drawl, but he's Kolehiyo-educated like any Kayuman noble.'

Panday cocked an eyebrow at Dangal. 'What? I *am* a southerner,' he said, laying on the drawl a little thicker so he was harder to understand. 'Besides, it's true. Your father might even have a hand in the Tuki invasion. Maybe killing off some banner houses he don't like, like say my House or House Payapa.'

'And you say that with complete certainty because?'

'Simple. King-man is not difficult to read. Youngest brother. Never meant to rule. Wife cheated on him. Stood on the sidelines in the last war. Inherits a kingdom that practically governs itself. He can hide who he is, but all that losing must have knocked a few screws loose in his head.'

'You don't paint a very flattering picture of our father, or our family for that matter,' Dangal said, bemused. 'But you're not wrong.'

'Hey, I'm your family, too, thanks to my adopted older brother Tulis.' Panday downed the contents of his cup. 'You, your majesty, if you're really leaving—which I think is politically dumb—you need to make your disappearance all mysterious-like if you don't want nobody chasing you across the country. Buy yourself some time to fix your affairs 'fore you take over from your Pa.'

Scowling, Dangal's mood visibly changed. 'I don't plan on returning.'

Dakila blurted out, 'Why in the Skyworld gods' names not?'

'Huh. Makes sense,' Panday said. 'You didn't strike me as the warmongering vendetta type.'

Dakila stared at him, aghast. 'You agree to this?'

'I don't,' Panday said firmly. 'Because then he'd be throwing my boy into the den of lions before he's ready.' He let out a strained breath, eyes on his empty glass. 'But it 'splains all that politicking he's been doing, riling up the Datus.

He's democratizing power so he doesn't need to go back.' Panday faced Dangal. 'How long you been planning this?'

'Long,' Dangal said simply.

'But the country needs a king, especially now in a time of war,' Dakila pleaded.

'If there's anything the Obsidian War has shown us, it's that we don't need a king to win wars. Just someone to lead the charge,' Dangal said.

'What about . . .' Dakila scrambled for words, any sort of reason to convince his brother to come back '. . . your duty to your country?'

'Duty is empty without love. My daughter is my duty. We've been searching for so long. Every time we think we've found her in some backwater seedplantation, we're proven wrong. That man who took my daughter and my wife, he's slippery. We know for sure where she is now. I'm not leaving this to chance again. I'm going to get her myself.'

'And after you retrieve your daughter?'

'I'll stay away, keep her safe from all this.'

Dakila opened his lips to speak, fury rising like a tide at dawn, slow and powerful at the same time.

'If I may intrude,' Panday said, accent gone and replaced by a formal city accent, eyeing the Dayo barmaid with golden hair hovering about. 'If you leave and Congress somehow forces the king to step down—which I'm telling you he is not likely to do without a fight—your absence will create a power vacuum that'll make the country vulnerable to dictators and invaders. All that work you did will be for nothing if we let outsiders take our country from us. You made a mess trying to even the playing field and create an exit for yourself—but you chose the wrong time for that, what with the Tuki coming down to wage war on us or the south threatening to secede from the country or the strangelords feeling like second-class citizens in their own country. Instead of a democratic government, you'll be handing off the country to some foreigner who doesn't have our interests at heart. And you and your daughter will always be a threat to any new ruler that dares to take power in Kayuman in the aftermath. You will never keep her safe by staying away.' His accent returned for the last part, saying, 'I hear no good things 'bout this Spider Empress woman. Frosty bitch, they say.'

Dangal clenched his jaw but capitulated, sighing and saying, 'Where did you find this joker, Dakila?'

Panday shrugged and gestured for the golden-haired Dayo barmaid to bring them another bottle of the yellow.

'It wasn't hard, *kuya*,' Dakila said, acknowledging the girl who placed a fresh bottle of the yellow on the table. 'He hangs out in taverns and bets on Magiting fights regularly like he has nothing to lose.'

'Hey! I won enough bets to actually own something lose-able,' Panday said, grabbing the bottle before any of them could get to it. ''Sides, Talim blood runs deep. I knew for sure you were my brother's son when I saw his face on you. The git's been chasin' after the queen even when they were wee children. Love did our House no good, did it?' He drank deep, straight from the bottle, letting out a big and loud exhale after, his breath charged with the nectarine-sweet scent of lost love, before adding, 'But what's life without love, right?'

# Chapter 26

## Yin

The Wind Goddess' wrath was swift and brutal. She did not linger on anger or hate. The Kayuman took and took and took till she was empty. She would never be empty again.

She began blowing out the fires that continued to eat Kanlungan and the stone houses around it, picking up Reds along the way and dumping them into a pile of humans under the tree.

They raised swords and sticks and stones, attempting in vain to bring her back down to the ground. She pulled the wind out of their bodies, strangling them, suffocating them, till the last man dropped to the ground, their faces purple and twisted in horror, death the last note on their faces.

Then she flew to the docks and pushed the ships away from her island, turning them askew, overturning them in the water, and slamming them against each other. She was the wind, she was the storm, she was the typhoon raging over the island, calling forth clouds and rain and thunder and lightning. Her wind sorted through men, women, and children, picking out the Reds and taking the wind out of their lungs methodically and dropping them into the ocean. Those that survived and were able to swim back to shore were met with a group of Dayo men who had realized quickly what Yin was doing.

It was over too quickly, and Yin looked out over the island, seeing the death she'd dealt in such a short time. How easy it was to take a life.

The rain soaked through her hair and her clothes. She should have been cold, but only a perverse calm remained, a relief that this part of her life was now over. That she could stop running again. That she could plant her feet firmly on the ground and not feel like her life was in danger.

She landed on the beach strewn with the dead Kayuman, their blood staining the white sand and the white foam-tipped waves ebbing and flowing from the ocean.

The Dayo survivors met her with reverence, kneeling before her, calling her names like Amihan, goddess, *diyosa*, saviour, like she did all that for them, them who treated her like an outcast, like she was the bane of their existence.

She saw Tiyago among them, kneeling, watching her warily as if waiting for punishment or condemnation.

She didn't do all this for them. She was neither Dayo nor Kayuman. She belonged nowhere. She owed these people nothing. She backed away from them, summoning the wind to catch her, lift her up, and take her away from this wretched island.

'Wait!' Tiyago called. 'Don't go, Yin!'

She turned to look at the beautiful red-haired boy and flashes of memory came to her, of cool nights on the beach, of frenzied joy at a town fiesta, of kindness when she felt alone. He wasn't going to turn her over to the Reds. Was it truly kindness if he had intended to use her for his own ends? Had she always been this naive?

'We tried to save your father, Yin,' Tiyago said, standing slowly, hands raised in surrender, looking up at her reverently. 'We really did, but when the Kayuman masters brought him out, he was already close to death.'

'Did you bring him to our home?'

'He asked to be brought there. He knew you'd come looking for him there.'

'He's dead. Galenya, too,' she said, trying and failing to keep the emotion out of her voice.

'Are you staying?'

She looked at each of the faces of the Dayo kneeling before her like she was some divine saviour. These were the same people who had treated her like an outcast for the person that she thought she was. It turned out that even she wasn't who she thought she was. She was far worse. Her father was not her real father. She wasn't just some girl from a backwater town. She was half-Kayuman, one who could wield seedmagic. And she wasn't just a seedmage. She was a godvessel.

She was a fable, a legend, and a myth.

But she was no hero. No divine saviour.

Her father, or the man she thought was her father, told her to wait here. Someone, her real father, was coming to save her, but how safe was the island? The Reds would be back and would probably send their worst to retrieve her. Surely, the better option would be to run away and find her father herself. But what would happen to these people when she left?

'Only long enough to keep the Reds away,' she said without thinking, echoing the very same words that her father—the man she thought was her father—said when they first landed here. 'Not any longer than necessary.'

She had nowhere else to go anyway but this island, no lead to her father other than here.

The rain fell as she gazed at the wretched people kneeling before her. Funny how she was always watching them like this, always separate from them, never one of them.

The wind cradled her in midair, gentle, warm, and comforting even under the pouring rain. The wind was not separate from her. The wind was her, and the wind was free.

She flew from the Dayo, from the dead Kayuman, from the remnants of the people she loved and the ruins of her home, and plunged deep into the mountain, following the path that always found her, that led her to her safe haven, her mountain, the place that had given her the wind.

* * *

# Epilogue

The Spider waits before she eats her prey. The woman paced in the hallowed hall of the Spider's temple, once built to commemorate her victories in war before it became her house of worship. Behind her was a giant block of ice, her ice, encasing swords, daggers, and knives of varying sizes, styles, shapes, and colours according to the power it gave its vessel, all suspended in time, tethering Jin and her siblings to its master, the Spider.

It was perennially cold inside; the white walls and domed roof were made to insulate ice and snow even in the warmer months. The blue glowlamps hanging from the ceilings cast an insidious light on all of them, especially the Spider, looking menacing and divine at the same time on an elevated altar. She stopped pacing and faced her *children*.

Jin and her *siblings* were kneeling before the altar, trying to make themselves look small and insignificant and inconsequential. If they played the Spider's game unquestioningly, if they were insignificant enough, then maybe they would be spared the Spider's wrath.

'Tell me you speak the truth,' the Spider said, paper-white skin practically glowing in the dark room, long black hair a cape of night sky cascading over her back as she paced, almond eyes black windows into a void. Her blade, a white rapier, long and thin, hung from her belt.

Jin knew that this would be one of those moments she'd remember all her miserable, immortal life. She was given a chance to preempt an incoming war, a chance to prolong her siblings' lives, a chance to save thousands of lives. But she had a thousand lives to choose from and she would trade it all for one life, one love, this life, this love. 'Yes,' Jin said.

Hanabi gasped. Seyo whimpered. Gamu let out a big breath. The others flinched but stayed silent otherwise. But they all kept their heads down. In the Lastan war, they had lost two siblings. Any one of them could be next.

'Spare us, please,' Hanabi pleaded to the humanity left in the Spider, her entire body trembling under the Spider's scrutinizing gaze. 'I'll fight for you. I'll do whatever you want.'

'Quiet, Hanabi,' Gamu said, resigned and defeated, without raising his head or looking away from the white-tiled floor. It had been a long time since the Spider had responded to something so mortal as begging, but then it had been an eternity since the Spider had been mortal. No living being held the memory of a mortal Spider. No one even remembered her true name.

Jin turned to Hanabi, her hands balling into fists at her sides, while the rest cowered where they knelt. Hanabi hadn't always been insufferable. This desperation to outlive them all only came after she watched the Spider eat her blood sister for her seedgod.

Jin sighed, a last attempt to assuage her guilt. 'Mother, please spare them. I'll lead the charge of war myself. I'll take your blade myself.'

Upon fusing souls with seedgods, seedmages were bound to the blades used to siphon divine magic into their bodies from the Skyworld. Whoever possessed their blades became the fused god's master, their will suspended in favour of their blades' wielder.

The Spider raised an eyebrow and walked long slow steps toward Jin. She pushed JinWun's head up so that they were looking at each other eye to eye. 'Always the compassionate one, you.' The Spider's eyes turned into dark, snake-like slits, white dots swirling with shards of light and colour of the other gods that lurk within her immortal form. With the wave of her hand toward the block of ice on the pedestal, she commanded the siblings to raise their arms to the side and present their hearts to her, to show her the black scar that their blades had left behind.

She pulled away and unsheathed her sword. The Spider's blade sang as it was pulled out of its ornate scabbard, webs of silver veins shining on the thin black surface of the metal. 'This death is necessary, my child.'

JinWun forced herself to keep looking at the Spider and the blade in her hand. She would not die a coward. She refused to die as an indentured servant who was so afraid that she had to turn away to the floor. She would die knowing that she had set into motion the Spider's death.

So, she looked at the woman, glared at her with all the rage and hatred she could muster. Her one regret had been allowing the Spider to control her heart when she had already controlled her will.

The Spider raised her blade up over her head, preparing to strike down. Jin braced herself, forcing herself not to look away from her death. She thought about her husband's face. He would be free of her soon. He would be free when the Spider finally got what she needed from Jin, after keeping him for decades in the dungeons.

And then the Spider smiled and patted Jin's cheek with her free palm before stabbing the blade straight through Seyo's heart next to Jin, pushing past skin, flesh, bone, spraying blood and gore out that side.

'No!' JinWun screamed, fighting to take back control over her body, fighting to free herself from the tether of the blades. Gamu was trying to do the same, while the others watched in equal parts horror and relief at what happened to their youngest.

Seyo held on to the blade piercing her chest, hands dripping blood around the thin blade, and looked to Jin, the shock registering late on her face as if she knew this was coming but did not expect the pain that came with it. Perhaps she knew. She had the magic to find out after all. Seyo's big, brown accusing eyes stared at JinWun, before glazing over into white, her lips moving to say, *'The shadows gather before the explosion of light.'*

Jin then watched the life go out of her eyes.

Pink light burst around the blade piercing Seyo's heart, surging through the veins of Spider's blade. The black metal morphed into a crystal rapier creating a conduit where magic flowed from Seyo to the Spider.

They knew it was over when they felt the Spider's hold on their tether loosen. They watched Seyo's blade disintegrate within the ice block, its light dimming within its shell. The blade slid out of Seyo's lifeless body, the crystal sword slick with red blood, concealing the magic swirling within it.

The Spider let go of her hold on their will and Jin went straight to Seyo's body, slowly disintegrating into ash now that the shell was emptied of its soul. The other siblings gathered around them with Gamu taking one of Seyo's small hands in his bigger one. They waited till the last fragment of Seyo's body drifted away before leaving, each one eyeing their blades encased in ice hungrily, wistfully, longingly. They could never take their blades back, even if they could get past the Spider's enchantments on the ice casing.

Freedom was a thing they gave up, for power itself was the chains that bound them. It was the thing withheld from them so long as their master refused to let go of the yoke. Freedom was a thing they had to fight for, to earn, to take back.

Jin stared at her hands, empty now without Seyo's body, even the blood that stained her skin and clothes gone. *Another person gone because of her selfishness.*

Seyo's power was an ability to see the future, to walk on paths yet to be taken, to see possibilities where there were none. Now, the Spider had that power, the power to shape the future according to her whims and to cheat at life where everyone had to live without knowing when they would die.

Jin couldn't help thinking that she'd be next, and the Spider was just taking her time with captured prey.

But she couldn't see the future, only the present and what must be done to survive another day.

'Now, my children,' the Spider said, sliding her sword back into the sheath hanging from her waist. 'We go to war.'

# Acknowledgements

It takes a lot of balls for a writer to think, 'Hey, I'm going to write a novel for the first time, so I'm going to write epic fantasy!' That thought would be akin to an indoor kitty-cat thinking it can take on a Bengal tiger in a fight. But it was in the middle of the lockdown, and I had a lot of time on my hands. Fortunately (or perhaps unfortunately), I literally don't have balls, and it only took me three long years, thirty-seven drafts, obsessive worldbuilding painstakingly handwritten in piles and piles of notebooks, and literally over a million words discarded to get to the manuscript that I finally pitched to publishers. Even then, I knew *Winds Of War* wasn't ready for the world to see. It took so much faith and patience for this book to come to fruition—not just from my part. I don't have the gall to say that I did it all alone. I have so many people to thank, it just might take another half a million words just to express my gratitude, and even then it might not be enough. Fortunately, I have the girl guts to try anyway.

Nora Nazarene Abu Bakar, Publisher of Penguin Random House SEA, you were the first to take a chance on me and my stories. I daresay you had more faith in *Winds Of War* than I ever did, and for that I am so very thankful. I hope my stories could live up—are living up—to that level of faith you had in me.

Thatchaayanie Renganathan, my wonderful, patient, and persistent editor, oh my god, I've made you so miserable these last few months. Where editing *Love On The Second Read* felt like a walk on the beach, editing *Winds Of War* felt like climbing a mountain with three peaks in the dead of night in the middle of a typhoon. Thank you, thank you, thank you so much for not giving up on me or my books. Thank you for staying with me till the third and last book in this trilogy. This trilogy would have still been a hot mess without you. I might stick to romance for the foreseeable future—or maybe not.

Chaitanya Srivastava, my publicist and best cheerleader and still a social media marketing genius, I will never forget that you called me in the middle of the night when I was in the middle of a panic attack (because I had just had my heart broken and I couldn't eat and I was out of prescription meds—it's a whole other thing) even when you weren't feeling so good yourself. Thank you so much for everything you've done for my books. We wouldn't be here without you. My books (and I!) would have faded into obscurity had you not dragged me out of the dark night of my soul.

Garima Bhatt, my digital media marketer, and Almira Ebio Manduriao, Head of Sales, thank you so so so much for all you do to get my books to bookstores and in readers' hands. I would have hoarded all my books to myself if you hadn't done what you've done.

Swadha Singh, Ishani Bhattacharya, Divya Gaur, and everyone who worked behind the scenes of making my books, hello again! I know what it's like to work in the background of making books, and sometimes I feel like my part of the job doesn't matter because it's not glitzy or nobody knows I was ever part of the project. Know that I see you! I know you're there! I will always remember that my book wouldn't exist without the hard work and love and patience you put into them. Thank you for all you do. We wouldn't be here without you.

Trisha Udumud, the book cover you made for *Winds of War* is just incredible! Thank you! Thank you so much for your patience and for your art and for just sharing your creativity with a noob like me. I daydream about the cover whenever I need a pick-me-up. I can't wait to see what you have in store for the next books!

Divya Gaur and Adviata Vats, I'm so sorry I had the gall to show you my messy, hot mess of map doodle, but thank you for making my made-up world look so, so, so much better. It has always been my dream to be scifi-fantasy author with a book that has fantasy map, and you made that dream come true for me. Thank you so much!

Mom, Dad, Jem, Jas, Lolamommy, Tita Jane, and my entire family, thank you for supporting my dream and for being understanding when I'm acting like an ogre when I'm smashing my keyboard to get in my daily word count goal. I hope you're proud of me.

Koko, June, James, Lio, Gem, Marc, Ela, Bea, Ms. Dina, Ms. Lotte, Ms. Rose, Ms. Jen, thank you for leaving me alone after I clock out so I can write my books (Haha!). It means so much to me that you gave me room to pursue my passions outside of the day job that I also love so much.

Mrs. Emerita Tagal, my favourite high school English teacher who tolerated my twenty-page essays for homework, can you believe that this is my second book? This wouldn't have happened if you hadn't believed I could write back when I actually couldn't write. Thank you for pushing me to pursue a career in writing even when the world had told me to pursue math instead.

The entire book community, Bookstragrammers and Booktokers and book bloggers and bookworms everywhere—you have been so generous and kind and loving and patient with me since my first book. Thank you for making all of those fun posts and for promoting my books on your platforms. Thank you for the time you put into reading, reviewing, commenting, and making posts!

And you, dear reader. It takes a lot of faith to pick up a book by a nobody from nowhere and read it all through the end. At the heart of the *Winds Of War* trilogy is an unabashed faith in love and in people's capacity to do everything in the name of love. It would then take real girl guts for me to say that it must be love that brought you here, because it was also an act of love that led me here to you. And in case you need to hear it now, I'll say it here: I love you. May your life be lived in love.